Traveling Through History

A Collection of Historical Short Stories

Janet Morrison

Cover designed by Janet Morrison using Bookbrush.com. Formatted by Janet Morrison using Atticus.io.

Contents

INTRODUCTION

The short stories in this collection were inspired by various means. Two were prompted by assignments in the writers group I used to belong to, while others grew out of genealogical research or personal experience. Others were written to introduce you to characters in the historical novels I'm writing.

My first attempt at writing a short story for publication was while I was a member of Queens Writers Group in 2002. Under the mentorship of our fiction writing instructor in the Continuing Education Department at Queens University of Charlotte, the group decided to dive into the new world of print-on-demand self-publishing. I wrote a short story, "The Tailor's Shears" for that book, *Inheriting Scotland*. I was a novice writer at the time, so you will be happy to know that I have edited the story for its inclusion in this collection of historical short stories.

The other stories in this book have been written over the ensuing 23 years.

"You Couldn't Help But Like Bob" grew out of research I have done about my mother's ancestors. It was interesting to learn that Robert Dooling was arrested several times in Colonial Virginia and, being in the days when there was no separation of Church and State, he was ordered to pay his fines in the form of tobacco paid to the Church of England.

"To Run or Not to Run" introduces you to another character who shows up in the historical novel I'm writing and who plays a major role in its sequel(s). George is a character who lives only in my imagination but the more time I spend with him, the more intrigued I am with him. I think you will become interested in George in "To Run or Not to Run" and I hope you will come to care deeply about him when you read my future historical novels.

"Making the Best of a Tragedy" introduces you to an important character in the historical novel I'm writing. Elizabeth Maxwell Gillespie Steele was a real person who owned and operated a tavern in Salisbury, North Carolina in the 1750s and 1760s. She lived an amazing life and I am eager for you to read the short story I wrote based on her life and flavored with some conversations she had in my imagination.

"From Scotland to Pennsylvania" was written as a result of the research I have done into my father's ancestry. I took the baptismal records of my great-great-great-great-grandfather and his two brothers, combined that information with the fact that they lived for a while in Pennsylvania after arriving from Scotland, and added lots of imagination to weave a fictional story of their journey.

"Whom Can We Trust?" was inspired by the local history story about a man who stood on the steps of the courthouse in Charlotte on May 20, 1775, and heard the Mecklenburg Declaration of Independence read. It is said that he went home and told his wife they needed to make a list of the people they could trust during the coming war.

I wrote "Go fight, Johnny!" after more genealogical research and discovering that I had ancestors who took part in the Battle of Kings Mountain because that's where they lived!

I wrote "A Letter from Sharpsburg" after discovering portions of several letters one of my great-grandfathers wrote to his parents and sister during the Civil War. He did not fight in the Battle of Sharpsburg, but I was inspired to write a fictional soldier's letter after reading about that battle.

I wrote the original version of "Slip Sliding Away" in 2003 for the second collection of short stories by Queens Writers Group, *Tales for a Long Winter's Night*, which was edited by Judith H. Simpson. It has gone through several revisions as I honed my fiction writing skills. The version in this book is the same version I published in 2023 as a stand alone short story. It is the same version visitors to my website receive when they subscribe to my newsletter.

I was inspired to write "A Plott Hound Named Buddy" because the North Carolina General Assembly named the Plott Hound the official state dog in 1989. I know a couple of people who are related to the Plott family that developed the Plott Hound in the mountains of North Carolina.

"Secrets of a Foster Child" was inspired by a local mission project at our church some years ago in conjunction with the Cabarrus County Department of Social Service.

"Ghost of the Battle of Guilford Courthouse" was my first attempt to write a ghost story. It grew out of some unexplainable occurrences in the condominium shared in the 1970s by my sister and another teacher. The condo was not far from where the Battle of Guilford Courthouse took place in 1781. I don't believe in ghosts, but some things defy logic.

"If This House Could Talk" was inspired by an old vacant farmhouse that stood less than a mile from where I grew up. While doing some local history and Rocky River Presbyterian Church history research, I learned that the family that lived in that house lost five sons in the Civil War. My Aunt Louise Morrison had planted the idea in my head to write a story from a house's point-of-view decades earlier when she wrote a story as if the house in which she grew up in the early 20th century was telling its memories.

I hope you will be entertained as you travel through history with the stories in this book.

Janet Morrison

THE TAILOR'S SHEARS

Author's Note:

This was my first published short story. Members of the Queens Writers Group (writers who had completed Judith Simpson's Fiction Writing course at Queens University of Charlotte) were invited in 2002 to submit their work to be included in a collection of short stories associated with Lochar Castle, a fictional castle of the Douglas Clan in Scotland. We were instructed to write a short story around an item found in the castle's keep. The story was to be told from the point-of-view of a member of the Douglas family. I wanted to include some of the history of the Covenanters. In a round-about way, that led me to choose a pair of tailor's shears for the item found in the castle keep.

The original version of this story, which was included in *Inheriting Scotland*, edited by Theresa Reilly Alsop, 2002, is a good example of what in fiction writing is called an "information dump." That's not a good thing! In rereading this story 21 years later, I was appalled at the writing – how little conversation it contained, as well as how I droned on and on as I attempted to give the history of the Covenanters and their plight in Scotland in the 1600s and early 1700s.

Never fear! I've taken my red pen to the original story. I edited and polished it for inclusion in *Traveling Through History: A Collection of*

Historical Short Stories. The story is told in the form of a document written by Sir Iain Douglas in the year 1703 as he reflected on his life and explained how the tailor's shears ended up in the castle. I hope you enjoy it.

Lochar Castle, Scotland
1703

These tailor's shears, no doubt, seem an odd relic to be stored away in Lochar Castle. One might wonder what connection common tailor's shears could possibly have with the Douglas clan. Not so long ago, these very cutting tools caused me to grapple with that age old dilemma that separates right from wrong. I am not proud of everything I've done in my life, but I believe in this instance I did the right thing in the end. I hope these shears and the story of my battle of conscience will serve to remind future generations of the Douglas clan to hold honour and friendship higher than politics.

Alexander Montgomery, a tailor in Solway, was the owner of the shears. He was the best tailor in the region, so the Douglas family used his services in spite of his religious beliefs. He was a Covenanter, and the older he got the more outspoken he became. He took great pride in his work and never let his convictions interfere with business.

Montgomery never once initiated a conversation about religion with me. He was a braw wee man in appearance with no distinguishing physical characteristics until 1685. A man of humble means, it was said that he had married above himself. His family lived in one room and he worked out of the other room in a small thatched roof stone building. The shelves in his shop were always neatly stacked with bolts of various fabrics, presenting a veritable riot of colour. He kept his threads, shears, and measuring tools in a drawer but had a nice wooden chest to transport those necessities when he was called upon to work at a location other than his shop, such as Lochar Castle or other customers' residences.

I was curious to know what made men like Montgomery continue to champion the Covenanting cause after so many years of persecution by the civil authorities. Life was difficult enough for a tailor with young children in a small village without his doing things to bring unnecessary hardship upon himself. One day in 1685, when I was in his shop being measured for a new suit of clothes, I asked him if we might discuss religion. It was just a few months after those two women over in Wigton were drowned for attending conventicles. The women knew it was unlawful for anyone to go to those illegal Presbyterian worship services out in the hills, but they went anyway.

In answer to my question, Montgomery said, "Ay, I suppose we could discuss religion, sir, if ye think it wise to do so." I was standing and Montgomery was down on his knees taking measurements. He kept busy with his work, careful not to look me in the eye.

I pursued the subject. "I don't have a clear understanding of what the Covenanters are about. I hear that you're one. And I hear that you thought it was wrong what happened over in Wigton. Is that true?"

"Ay, it is true," he said. "I believe any thinking man would disapprove —" He stopped without finishing the sentence and cleared his throat. "And what is it you would like me to explain?"

"Just why is it the Covenanters cannae compromise and make peace with the King? Back forty years ago in my military days, I thought I had a fairly good idea of what the Covenanters stood for, but with the passage of time I have grown somewhat weary of it all and wonder if the present-day Covenanters even know what they're fighting for or against."

Montgomery's face turned red as a beetroot and his blue eyes blazed. As he stood up, he snapped the measuring tape with his two hands and jerked it around his shoulders in typical tailor fashion. I could tell it was all he could do to control himself and not lash out at me. My eyes searched his work table for his tailor's shears, a dirk, or anything else that could be used as a weapon, in case he lost his temper and temporarily forgot his place. For a moment I thought perhaps I had said too much. Though I was several inches taller than Montgomery, he was a younger man and in better physical condition than I.

"Make peace with the King?" Montgomery asked through nearly clenched teeth. "Forgotten what we're fighting for? Surely you are not serious, sir!"

I assured him that I was serious.

Montgomery took a couple of deep breaths and calmed himself before answering. "My good sir," he said, "We believe that Jesus Christ is the head of the church."

I reminded him that the King believes he is the head of the church, even though he obviously needed no reminding.

"There is no room for compromise on such an issue," he said. "If you will recall, sir, Charles I decreed that only Episcopalians could hold office in Scotland. Things became so desperate that the National Covenant was drawn up. The Presbyterian ministers were put out of their churches. The people were charged as being rebels, which was an offence punishable by death."

I assured him that I knew my Scottish history.

"Sixty thousand people went to Edinburgh to sign the Covenant," he said. "When I think of the stand those men took that day...." Montgomery's voice trailed off and his gaze showed that his thoughts had transported him to Greyfriars Churchyard. It was as if he had been there himself to sign the document. His voice became strong again and his words were chosen carefully. "They gathered there at Greyfriars after a day of fasting. One-by-one the church leaders stepped forward to sign it. Some pricked a finger and signed in blood. Others added the words, 'until death' after their names. They were signing their own death warrants, and they knew it! If we do not continue to fight for religious freedom, they all died in vain."

I asked him what made him keep fighting. After forty years, I thought there must be more to it than protecting the honour of those men.

"We keep fighting because we believe in our cause with every fibre of our being," he said. "We believe it down to our very souls."

"But don't you see your cause is hopeless?" I asked.

"Hopeless?" he almost shouted. "If ye think the Covenanters are without hope, then ye really do not understand at all, sir. Surely, ye remember when Charles I was beheaded. Our disagreement with him was strictly in matters of religion. We never stopped supporting him as king in civil matters. We crowned Charles II king at Scone and had high hopes for him. He signed the Covenant but he immediately started trying to destroy the Presbyterian Church of Scotland."

I was getting tired of his insinuating that I didn't know our country's history, so I told him some of my life story – how I joined Montrose after the Battle of Kilsyth in August of 1645, just two years after the Solemn League and Covenant was signed. I told him that a month after Kilsyth I was with the Royalist troops at Philiphaugh when we were, shall I say, surprised by the Covenanters' cavalry. I barely escaped with my life! I told him he didn't need to lecture me about the forties. I was eighteen years old in the king's army, and I was in the thick of it. Raising my voice more than I should have, I said, "You, I believe, were still a babe clinging to your mother's skirts."

It was at that time that I noticed a slight movement in the cloth curtain in the doorway that separated Montgomery's workshop from his family's living quarters. I saw his wife and two children peeping around the curtain, no doubt trying to see who was arguing with their husband and father. Catching my eye, the woman quickly closed the curtain and I heard her tell the children to move back. Not finished, I turned my attention back to Montgomery and said, "Do not pretend to lecture me!"

I thought I noted just a hint of a bow of his head as he apologized and told me he meant no disrespect to me personally. Then he paid his respects to Montrose, calling him a turncoat. He said something about not having any respect for a man who tries to play both sides of the fence.

I agreed with him, but he continued to run down Montrose. "He got what he deserved in the end," Montgomery said, "his head on a spike in Edinburgh."

"Ay," I said, "but I still want to know what your motives are." I asked him what made him so passionate for his cause. By then I was toying with him a wee bit, which I later came to regret.

"All we want is to be left alone to worship as we please," Montgomery said.

"I see," I said. "That seems little enough to ask."

"Ay," he said. "So little, and yet so much. That is all the two women in Wigton wanted. And to think, they were tied to stakes and the tide came in higher and higher until they drowned. And how brutal and vulgar the things the officers said to them as the cold waves crashed upon them. Is there no decency in the country?"

I looked away. There seemed to be nothing for me to say to him. I couldn't defend the drowning of the two women. Montgomery stooped and returned to his measuring. There was an uneasy silence between us until he finished his work.

"I believe I have all the measurements I need," he said. He asked if I needed anything else, and I didn't know of anything.

"I'll bring your suit to Lochar. It will mayhap be a week," he said. I turned to take my leave.

"Good day, sir," Montgomery said, as I opened the door.

"Good day," I said, not looking back. I pulled the door closed and gathered my collar up around my neck against the chill wind and drizzle. I got in my carriage to return to Lochar.

As I rode back home, I thought about some of the things Montgomery had said, and I wondered what made a man so steadfast in his convictions – religious or otherwise – that he would risk his life for them. I asked myself what I would be willing to die for, and all I could think of were my wife and daughter.

The rain had stopped by the time I reached Lochar and, upon arriving at the castle, I found my sixteen-year-old daughter, Fiona, in the arms of her beau. He was a Campbell and a soldier, and I was not pleased with the situation. I had an uneasy feeling about the man's integrity when it came to matters of civil conduct while in the king's service and, therefore, the way he conducted his personal life. I cleared my throat as I approached the couple.

"Sir Iain," Robert Campbell said, releasing the rather tight hold he had on my daughter. Fiona quickly tried to secure loose strands of her waist-length red hair pulled back from her face and hanging in natural waves down her back. She was the very image of her mother when I met her twenty-two years earlier.

"I did not hear you arrive, sir," Campbell said. "How are you keeping, sir?"

I assured him that I was well and decided to have a wee bit of fun at his expense. "I see you're doing well, also," I said. Fiona blushed as she continued to fumble with her hair, and Campbell seemed to not know what to say next. "Do you not have duties to attend to this afternoon, Mr. Campbell?"

"Ay. Ah. Ah. No," he stammered.

"What sort of answer is that for a soldier?" I asked.

Fiona's face was ablaze in anger now, but she had the good sense to keep silent.

"No, sir," Campbell said, mustering his most confident soldier voice. "I am not on duty until tonight, sir."

"It is time for you to leave, Mr. Campbell," I said. "Come inside, Fiona," and I started into the castle.

"Yes, Father," Fiona said, but she did not come right away.

My wife, Margaret, met me as soon as I got inside. "What was that all about?" she asked, ushering me over to the fireplace. There was a roaring, crackling fire and it felt good to warm my hands by it.

"I interrupted something," I said. "They did not even hear me as I approached. As Fiona's mother, you need to speak to her about her behaviour and the company she keeps. I believe she forgets her station. And there is just something I don't like about that young man."

"Is the thing you don't like about him the fact that he likes your daughter?" she asked as she struggled to reach up with both hands to rub my neck and shoulders. Her hands were bent and stiff with a disease that kept her joints red, swollen, and painful, especially in cold and damp weather. Of course, cold and damp weather is all we have here in Scotland, or so it seems.

"No, there's more to it than that," I said. "I don't trust the man. He has trouble looking me in the eye. That is not a good trait in a man – a man in the king's army. I don't want Fiona to see him again."

"Perhaps you're being too hard on him," Margaret said. "Let's bide our time. Perhaps things will work out as you wish."

"You are younger than I, my dear. I have seen things you cannae imagine. And things are so much more so with Fiona. I would like to think I could trust her judgement, but I'm more than a wee bit worried. The lass is so like you, Margaret – so trusting. And she is becoming a bonnie young lady, also so like her mother. She has your lovely red hair and green eyes."

"But she has your temper," Margaret said, "and I fear it will be her ruination someday. She does not know when to hold her tongue."

I don't know how much of our conversation Fiona heard, for the next thing I knew she rushed past us and up the stairs without a word. Her chamber door slammed shut, and I must admit there was a distance between us for several days thereafter.

***

The next time I saw Alexander Montgomery was the next week when he brought the suit of clothes for me to try. He came to my office and then I led him upstairs to my chambers. He was very professional that day as I tried on the suit. He checked it over meticulously, as always, making sure it hung just so. I knew his outspokenness, particularly since the incident in Wigton, would sooner or later bring the wrath of the civil authorities down on the man. I don't think he wished to discuss religion with me again but, before he left, I asked if I might have a personal word with him. He hesitated but then agreed.

"Do you not think you're too outspoken in your views?" I asked.

"No, sir," he said. "It is my way."

"Should you not hold your tongue sometimes? Think of what would become of your wife and children should something unfortunate happen to you."

Montgomery turned pale. "Are you threatening my family, sir?" he asked.

"No. Of course not. I have no reason to wish harm on you or your family. I only have your and your family's welfare in mind."

"I appreciate your concern, sir, but a man has to be true to himself. I couldn't live with myself if I stood idly by and let these persecutions continue without trying to stop them. And do not worry about my wife and children. It would be better for them to live without me, knowing I had stood up for what was right, than to live with me knowing I was a coward. And now, sir, is there anything else today?"

"No," I said. "That is all."

Montgomery gathered his things and took his leave. I had an overwhelming feeling that would be the last time I would ever see him. I had done all I could for him. After all, I had warned him that he was traveling down a dangerous path.

Days passed and I heard nothing of Montgomery, though there were rumours that local Covenanters were being singled out and punished in various ways. An iron device called "the boot" was one form of torture being used to try to get Covenanters to give the civil authorities the information or oaths they desired. The boot held a man's leg firmly in place while another man crushed his knee joint using an iron wedge and a sledgehammer. Ghastly!

***

A fortnight passed and the rumours of attacks on Covenanters in the area continued. I heard that Montgomery had been arrested. I hoped it wasn't true.

At the same time, my concerns about Robert Campbell would not go away. He called upon Fiona several times, and after his last visit she seemed upset but would not tell Margaret or me why. I believed Campbell had said or done something to cause this and I decided I must confront him.

One afternoon when he came to call upon Fiona, I went with her to meet him at the door. We exchanged greetings and I invited him inside. I could tell that Fiona was uneasy, no doubt wondering what I was going to say next.

"I would like to have a word with you in private, Mr. Campbell. Excuse us, Fiona, while Mr. Campbell and I go to my office. We shouldn't be too long. Come with me, Mr. Campbell."

"Ay, sir," Campbell said. Fiona gave me a worried look but said not a word.

Campbell and I walked through the entry hall and grand foyer and into my office. I invited him to sit down.

"What is it you want to discuss, sir?" he asked.

"Fiona has been upset since your last visit. Can you tell me why that is?"

"No, sir. I don't know."

"Are you certain? Did the two of you have an argument?"

"No, sir. Excuse me, sir, but perhaps you should ask Fiona these questions and not me."

"Very well," I said, and the young man stood up as if to leave. He was tall and muscular for his age, and I believe in his immaturity he thought he might intimidate me with his superior size.

"Sit back down," I said. "We are not finished. What do you think about the tactics being employed against some of the citizens in the area?"

"I'm afraid I don't know what you're referring to, sir. Perhaps I should be going, since I'm unable to answer any of your questions." He stood again and started toward the door.

"Sit back down! I will tell you when our conversation is finished. Are you unable or unwilling to answer my questions? I think you know exactly what tactics I'm talking about."

"If you're referring to the treatment of the Covenanters—"

"Ah, so you do know," I said.

"Sir, I have orders and I have to follow them."

"Ay," I said. "I served in the king's army myself. I know all about following orders and what happens to those who do not. I did not ask you if you followed orders. I asked you what you think about the tactics being used."

The young soldier was silent. As usual, he would not look me in the eye. "Surely you have an opinion," I said. There was no response. "I would not look favorably upon my daughter being courted by a young man who did not have an opinion on such a thing."

"I do have an opinion, sir, but I don't believe a soldier should discuss such things with those not the army," he said. His face flushed a wee bit. "Is there anything else today, sir, or am I free to go?"

"You may go," I said. He stood and turned to leave, but when he got to the door he stopped and turned back toward me and asked, "May I continue to court your daughter, sir?"

"Ay, for now. But if I were you, I would find a way to answer my question before not much more time passes."

"Ay. Good day, sir."

"Good day, Robert."

***

Imagine my surprise just three days later when Mrs. Montgomery and her children appeared at Lochar seeking my assistance. There were dark circles under their eyes – even the wee lass. Mrs. Montgomery's eyes were red and swollen from crying, though she kept a stiff upper lip while in my presence. She spoke and carried herself well, which left me to believe that she had enjoyed a good upbringing.

"I'm not accustomed to begging, sir," Mrs. Montgomery said. She pulled her children closer. The lad appeared to be about four years old and the wee lass perhaps two. The strain and embarrassment showed on Mrs. Montgomery's face. She looked as though she had not slept in a week. The wee lass was too young to understand where she was or why she had been brought to the castle. She was visibly fearful. She trembled from time to time and sucked on her thumb as silent tears dripped off her chin. I believe the lad saw the experience as an adventure. His eyes darted from one thing to another in my office. He seemed quite content until his gaze fell upon the broadsword on the wall. It seemed to scare the lad.

"Go on, Mrs. Montgomery," I said after observing her and the children for several minutes. I was finding this interruption to be very irritating and was eager for the woman to state her business.

"My husband, Alexander Montgomery, has been your tailor for many years," she said.

"Ay, since around 1665. And his father was my tailor before him."

"Are you aware that my husband has been taken away?"

"I heard rumours."

"Last week soldiers burst into his shop and roughed him up. They shouted obscenities at him for being a Covenanter. I came running from the other room to see what was happening. As they dragged him out the door, one of the soldiers yelled back at me, 'You forget everything you saw and heard, or you'll be sorry!' I watched from the window as they dragged my husband down the street. A small crowd gathered. One of the soldiers snatched the shears out of Alexander's hand and, to my horror, cut off both his ears! The soldiers laughed. Then Alexander was led away, blood running down from his head."

Mrs. Montgomery stopped to blow her nose with a handkerchief she had been wringing in her hands. "Forgive me, sir, but this is not easy." She choked back tears, making a valiant effort to regain her composure.

I told her to continue when she was ready. After a couple of minutes, she spoke. "I have been told that my husband is being held by the army with other prisoners until a ship comes to take them to the West Indies. I beg for your mercy, sir. You are a man of great power and influence. If you could make it possible for my husband to be released, I would be forever grateful and in your debt."

"There really is not anything I can do. I'm sorry that your husband's beliefs and actions have brought such suffering upon you and your children, but he knew the risks."

"Ay, sir, he knew the risks, but surely you don't think he should be banished to the West Indies for not bowing to King Charles as head of the church. And surely you don't think he could keep silent over the unspeakable injustice done last spring in Wigton."

"I'm not here to debate the fine points of religious and civil liberties with you, my good lady. Now, if there is nothing else you wish to ask of me today –"

"No, sir. There is nothing else. Come, weans," she said as she rose from her chair, her arms gathering her two children close. As she walked out of my office, she thanked me for hearing her out.

Hoping that was the last I would hear of Alexander Montgomery or his family, I returned to my desk to attend to matters of business. The image of Mrs. Montgomery and those two wee children kept intruding my thoughts, though, for the remainder of the afternoon.

At our evening meal, I had little appetite. I was quite distracted, to the point that Margaret asked me several times what was troubling me. I pushed my plate away. "Does it have anything to do with Mrs. Montgomery's visit this afternoon?" she asked. "I met her as she left. She was quite disappointed that you seemed unable to help her. What if that were me and our weans in such a predicament? Would you not want someone of influence such as yourself to help us?"

I did not look at my wife or answer her.

Fiona broke the silence. "I have—I have been meaning to say something to you about what was done to Mr. Montgomery." She looked at her mother, as if I weren't there.

"How do *you* know what was done to Mr. Montgomery?" Margaret asked.

"Robert. Robert knows," Fiona stammered. "Robert was the one who cut off Mr. Montgomery's ears."

"No! What a ghastly thing to do!" Margaret said, rising from her chair and clutching her napkin to her mouth. I thought she might get sick.

I reached out and laid my hand on Fiona's arm. "How do you know that?"

"Because he told me what he did. He was bragging. In fact, he led me to believe he had done it to impress me, though, in truth it sickens me," Fiona said.

"You know how young men like to brag to impress each other or a lass," Margaret said. "Surely, Robert had nothing to do with it." She sat down.

"Yes, I fear he did," Fiona looked at her mother and then at me. "He brought me something to prove it." Tears spilled down her cheeks and she bit her lower lip.

"Whatever could he have as proof?" Margaret asked.

"Mr. Montgomery's tailor's shears. He gave me the shears," Fiona said, her mouth drawn up in a manner which revealed a high level of disgust.

I could no longer keep my seat. I commenced to pace around the room. "Only a coward does such a thing to an unarmed man!" I shouted. "And only a brute gives a young lass such a gift. The bastard! I told you Robert Campbell was not good for you. Ach! Why did you not tell us about the shears and what Robert told you? Your mother and I have been asking you what was wrong, but you would not tell us. Oh, lass, why could you not tell us? When did this happen?" I grasped the end of the dining table and leaned in toward Fiona.

"It was last week. I couldn't bring myself to admit to you that Robert would do such a thing. I couldn't admit it to myself. I love him. At least I did love him. I thought I loved him. I didn't know what to do. Robert said something I didn't understand. He said, 'Perhaps your father will be happy now. Perhaps he will think I'm good enough for you now.' What did he mean by that? You wouldn't want such a thing to be done to Mr. Montgomery." Her eyes pleaded for answers.

"No, my dear, I would not want something like that done to Mr. Montgomery," I said. "I believe Robert came to the wrong conclusions concerning my views about the treatment of the Covenanters, but he will not blame me for his actions. He is nothing but a coward.

He is a dangerous man, Fiona, and I forbid you to see him again. I will go to his commander in the morning."

"But you cannae report him," Fiona said. "You can't."

"I have no choice but to report him. He will be lucky if I see his commander before I see him," I said.

"But he said this would be our little secret and, if I told anyone, I would be sorry."

"How dare he!" Margaret said. "Iain, you must do something!"

"I will be at the encampment at first light," I said. "Fiona, did he indicate how he would hurt you?"

"No, sir."

"Has he ever hurt you?" I asked.

"No, not really."

"That sounds like a 'yes' to me," I said.

"What has Robert done to you?" Margaret asked her.

"He has bruised my arms on occasion."

"He's hurt you and you never told us?" I asked. "And you have continued to see him? And I have invited him into my office?"

"Yes, sir." Tears rolled down Fiona's cheeks as Margaret came around the table and put her arm around her.

"I asked him if he knew why you were upset, but he denied knowing anything," I said. "Wait until I see him again! He will wish he had never laid eyes on you, and he will most certainly wish he had never lied to me!"

"Calm down," Margaret said.

"Woman, do not tell me to calm down. Do you not see what is happening? Fiona, where are the shears?"

"I hid them in my room."

"Bring them to me. Now. Now!" I said.

Fiona hurried from the dining hall and returned shortly holding the shears out ahead of herself with her thumb and forefinger. It was obvious she did not fancy touching them. I took the shears from her, and she asked to be excused for the remainder of the evening.

With Fiona upstairs and out of earshot, Margaret asked me what I was going to do with the shears. I told her I would put them out of sight in my office for now.

"I hope we've seen the last of Robert Campbell," Margaret said.

"Fiona has seen the last of him, but he hasn't seen the last of me," I said.

***

Before first light the next morning, I rode to the army's encampment and asked to have a word with the commanding officer. He was outraged upon hearing that one of his men had threatened my daughter, and he assured me that he would not tolerate such behaviour from his men. I asked if I might have a word with Campbell, and he was called out to see me.

"How good to see you, Sir Iain," Campbell said. "What can I do for you today?"

"Do not taunt me with your false pleasantries," I said. "You lied to me the day I asked you why Fiona was upset. You have hurt her. You have given her a weapon of mutilation as a present and have threatened her with more violence if she told anyone!"

"Those are strong accusations, sir," Campbell said.

"I have the proof I need," I said. "I forbid you to ever see my daughter again, though in truth, she does not desire to see you again. You are not to come to Lochar Castle. You are not to try to make conversation with Fiona or my wife, if they ever have the misfortune of meeting up with you in the village or elsewhere. Have I made myself clear?"

"Ay, sir, you have," Campbell said.

"Good," I said, and I turned and walked back to my carriage. As I drove away, I glanced over my shoulder to see the young soldier still watching me. I do believe he stared at me until I was out of sight. He was, no doubt, very angry.

Alexander Montgomery's situation haunted my thoughts as I returned to Lochar. Though I felt some degree of loyalty to the man due to our long association, I could not overlook our religious differences. The Covenanters had been warned for many years about what would happen to them if they did not submit to the king's demands in religion. Montgomery had a good business, was respected in the village, had a pleasant wife and two wee children. He had much to lose, but I had even more to lose if I tried to help him.

I could not shake the images of Montgomery being dragged down the street and mutilated or of his wife and children sitting before me, imploring me to save him. Montgomery's words from our last conversation still ring in my ears. "Do not worry about my wife and children," he said. "it would be better for them to live without me, knowing I had stood up for what was right, than to live with me knowing I was a coward." Bold words from a brave man. Time was quickly running out for him, though. Deep down, I knew it.

The next morning, Margaret asked me what I had decided to do about Montgomery.

"I cannae help him," I said. "I may have to answer to God for it someday, but I cannae forget Philiphaugh. I nearly lost my life fighting those Covenanters in '45. I cannae turn my back on my past."

"Can you turn your back on Alexander Montgomery?" she asked me.

The question cut me to the bone. "There is nothing I or anyone else can do to help him now," I said.

"You might be able to turn your back on Mr. Montgomery, but I cannae turn my back on his wife and children," she said. "As soon as we get Fiona's situation with Robert Campbell resolved, I must do something to help those children."

"I don't know what we can do for them," I said. "I am going into the village on business. I shall be back late in the afternoon."

"We must do something!" I heard as I rode off into the fog.

When I arrived in the village, there was a great commotion in the street. I inquired why there was such a boisterous crowd and was told that a group of prisoners had been stripped, roped together in pairs, and marched off to Leith. They were Covenanters. There would be a ship waiting in Leith to take them to Barbados. I felt sick to my stomach. I knew Montgomery was in the group and his fate was sealed. I hoped his wife would not see me, if she were in the crowd. I did not wish to be confronted by her. But, being a small village, there was little chance we could avoid seeing one another.

I finished my business as quickly as possible and tried to get on the road ahead of the angry mob, but it was not to be. Soldiers lined the streets, but it was all they could do to contain the Covenanters and their sympathisers. I was pushed, jabbed, and insulted as I moved along. Women and children were wailing and old men were shouting in anger between sobs. I tried to force my way down the street before violence broke out between the mob and the soldiers. My carriage was finally in sight, when one voice rose above the roar of the crowd.

"Sir Iain!"

I stopped in my tracks and slowly turned to see Montgomery's wife, though she was hardly recognizable. If anything, she looked more haggard than she did when we first met at Lochar. She tightly held onto her children, one in each hand. They were worse for the wear as well, though I had the feeling that all three had dressed in their finest clothing that day to say goodbye to husband and father. The wee lass looked upon me with a horror in her eyes that I will never forget. The lad merely stared at me.

"Sir Iain," Mrs. Montgomery repeated. "May I have a word with you, please, sir?"

I am afraid my countenance revealed my hesitancy to agree, but I gathered my resolve and suggested that we might have a word in private beside my carriage. I pointed to it and she and her children joined me there.

"Sir Iain," she began, and she grabbed my forearm and knelt on her knees as if begging. "My husband was marched off today. He is to be taken to the West Indies. I am so afraid for him! Ye know what happened to that ship of Covenanters off the coast of Orkney a few years ago. Two hundred of them drowned when the ship wrecked!"

"Yes, madam, I remember."

"Sir Iain, please do something!" Then, obviously embarrassed by her outburst, she stood up and calmly said, "I beg of you, sir, if you ever have occasion to know of my husband's whereabouts or the conditions under which he is being held, or if you should ever have the opportunity to make it possible for him to come home, my weans and I would be forever in your debt. I beg of you, sir." With that, she lowered her eyes, bowed her head to me, thanked me for hearing her out, and disappeared into the noisy crowd before I could speak.

***

In the weeks that followed that incident, the image of that woman and her children haunted me. I knew I was going to have to do something to aide her, but I did not yet know what or how. As has often happened in my life, my wife prodded me.

"I've been thinking about the Montgomery family," Margaret said to me one evening as we sat by the fire. She stared into the flames as they leapt from log to log. It was a windy night and there was a strong draft up the chimney. "When it's cold like this, I think about those children. They are never dressed warmly. The cobbler's children never have shoes, and the tailor's children never have adequate clothing. I know Mrs. Montgomery is doing the best she can for them, but they must be awfully cold and hungry."

"Ay, I suspect so," I said.

"I have a plan," Margaret said. "I want to take some food and clothing to them."

"I suppose there is nothing wrong with that. I am going into the village in the morning. I could deliver the things then."

"Oh, no, dear. It would be unseemly for you to be seen coming and going from Mrs. Montgomery's house with Mr. Montgomery away. It would be much more acceptable for me to make all future contact with her."

"Very well," I said. "You are correct. Take what money you need and buy the children some clothes. I cannae help Mr. Montgomery. Perhaps it will ease my conscience to know that we are helping his children."

"Until he returns."

"Until he returns?" I asked. "You sound as if ye think the man is merely away on business. He is gone forever, Margaret. Have you ever heard of a banished Covenanter coming back home? I think not."

Throughout the fall and winter, my wife took food and articles of clothing for the children to the Montgomery home. The cold winds were relentless in the winter of 1685-1686, and the children did not have suitable clothing. It was in early April, after Margaret's third or fourth visit to the Montgomery home in the new year that she came home and reported that she had been watched by a soldier.

"I cannae be sure," she said, "but I think it was Robert Campbell."

"I was afraid he had not forgotten us," I said. "No doubt, he has revenge on his mind. You mustn't go to see Mrs. Montgomery again. It is not safe."

"I cannae just stop going. Not without telling her why. Surely the king's army has better things to do than harass a woman going to visit a friend."

"I'm telling you it is not safe," I said. "You are not just a woman visiting a friend. You are Fiona's mother and my wife going to visit and lend aid to the wife of a banished Covenanter. Campbell is still angry with me, and the best way to hurt me is to hurt you or Fiona. By his own admission, we know he is capable of heinous acts. Promise me you will not do anything more to put yourself in danger."

Margaret promised.

***

In September, 1686, my sources told me that the ship Alexander Montgomery was on arrived safely on the island of Barbados. Though several of the men succumbed to disease and were buried at sea, I was assured by the authorities that Montgomery survived the voyage.

"We must get the news to Mrs. Montgomery," Margaret said, as soon as I told her. "Can we go tonight? I have not visited her since the day I was watched. Surely, we can go and tell her this. It would give me an opportunity to take the children some things."

"Very well," I said, for I knew my wife would find a way to get to Mrs. Montgomery, with or without my blessing. "I shall go with you in the carriage."

Though forbidden to visit the Montgomery's home again, Margaret had continued to purchase fabric and make clothing for the children in hopes of someday being able to deliver the items. I often chided her, but she insisted that the sewing was good for her stiff fingers. While I had the carriage brought around, Margaret gathered the pieces of clothing together and wrapped them securely in a blanket. She also filled a small basket with pastries.

That evening we went to the Montgomerys' house. I took the bundle of clothes out of the carriage and accompanied Margaret to the door. Mrs. Montgomery was delighted to see my wife again and the two children could not hide their joy. But it was obvious that Mrs. Montgomery was not well. She had a terrible cough and one could hear a wheezing sound with every breath she took. Her face had the look of someone quite a bit older than I knew her to be, and her formerly beautiful brown hair was nearly white. I had never seen anyone age so quickly.

Margaret reached into her basket and pulled out two fresh scones oozing with melted butter and jam. I do not know who enjoyed the scene more -- the children devouring the pastries, my wife and Mrs. Montgomery watching them, or me as I had the pleasure of seeing all four of them so happy, if only for a few minutes.

I placed the bundle on the floor in front of where Mrs. Montgomery sat. I untied the twine around the blanket and stepped back to watch Margaret's and Mrs. Montgomery's excitement over the contents. Mrs. Montgomery was very appreciative of the blanket and the clothing, holding each garment up to admire it.

But Margaret could wait no longer for Mrs. Montgomery to learn the true reason for our visit. "We have news for you," Margaret said. She turned to me and nodded for me to tell Mrs. Montgomery what I had learned that day.

"My sources tell me that your husband arrived safely in the island of Barbados after five months at sea. The crossing was stormy and many men did not survive the voyage, but I have been assured that your husband arrived safe and sound."

"What is he doing? What else can you tell me?" Mrs. Montgomery asked, tears streaming down her face. The children had finished eating and now gathered around to find out why their mother was crying.

"These are tears of joy, weans," she said. "Your father is alive!"

"When is he coming home? When is he coming home?" they cried.

"Not now," she said. "I do not know when. Go play. I need to talk to Sir Iain and Lady Douglas for a wee while."

She turned back to me. "What else can you tell me?"

"That's all I know," I said. "For my family's safety – and yours --, it is not good for me to ask any more questions at this time or show too much interest in the Covenanters. Suspicions about any ties I might have with the rebels, or to your husband, would not be in my favour. In fact, my wife and I are taking some risks by coming here tonight."

"You mean you are in danger?" she asked.

"Ay," Margaret said. "The last time I visited you, I was watched by a soldier. That is why I have not come back until tonight. And I do not know when it will be safe for me to come again."

Mrs. Montgomery gasped. "I am so sorry! I had no idea. I never considered that any personal harm could come to you because you had befriended me in my time of need. Please, you must go before anyone sees you. I will keep you in my prayers until we can safely meet again. Thank you for all you have done for us. I will never forget you. Come weans. Come say goodbye to Sir Iain and Lady Margaret and thank them for your gifts."

We stood to leave, and the children came running. My wife hugged both children. Mrs. Montgomery said goodbye and we left the wee cottage. When we stepped outside, I quickly looked up and down the street. Although I did not detect anyone watching us, one can never be too sure of such things. I had an uneasy feeling as Margaret and I got into the carriage. We started back to the castle. The horses' hooves made an unmistakable noise as we rode over the cobblestones. We rode along in silence, both of us left with our own private thoughts. A part of me hoped that Mrs. Montgomery would move away and I could still get rid of that problem.

***

Before long I heard that Mrs. Montgomery had moved in with relatives because she did not have the means to continue on in the cottage with her husband's shop, but she remained in the village and our paths crossed from time to time. Unlike on the day of her husband's departure, when she accosted me, in our future meetings she always waited for me to speak to her first. She showed a surprising degree of wisdom in how she conducted herself. It, no doubt, gave Montgomery great comfort in his days of confinement across the sea to know that his wife was such an independent spirit and resourceful enough to take care of herself and their children.

With the passing months, more stories circulated about the lucrative sugar cane business in the West Indies. There was good money to be made from the sugar and the rum coming out of the islands. After some careful study and consideration, I invested in the Barbados Sugar and Rum Company in July of 1687. Business was good and profitable. I saw it as merely a good business venture, but my wife saw it as an opportunity for me to secure the release of Alexander Montgomery, or at least to ascertain his condition. I was not eager to become entangled in the Covenanter's affairs again, but Margaret was persistent.

It was necessary for me to travel to Edinburgh to sign some papers in connection with my investments. I did not want to go to Edinburgh because there was so much unrest in the country. I cautioned Margaret and Fiona not to tell anyone that I was going away, but my fears regarding their safety were realized when I returned home just three days later. When I arrived at Lochar Castle, I found Margaret more distraught than I had ever seen her in all our twenty years of marriage.

"Robert Campbell was here!" she said.

"When? Why? Were you hurt? Was Fiona harmed?"

"No, just frightened. He came last night and beat on the door. It was around midnight."

"Where was the sentry?

"He was sick with the bloody flux and had gone to relieve himself. That is how Robert was able to gain entry to the grounds."

"What happened?"

"Fiona and I came downstairs where we were joined by the maids. I believe Robert was drunk. I told him through the closed door to leave. He shouted insults at us and many slurred words we could not understand. After a few minutes, he left."

"Where is Fiona now?"

"Upstairs in her room sound asleep. We are both exhausted from the ordeal and not getting to sleep until after daybreak."

"I am going to the encampment," I said. "I should be back before dark."

"No, you mustn't go," Margaret said. "The one thing I understood him to say was, 'You forget everything you saw or heard, or you'll be sorry.' With you here, I doubt he will come back. Please do not go over there and start something. We have had enough trouble already."

"Are you positive it was Campbell?

"Fiona is. She recognized his voice, but it would just be our word against his if he were questioned. Please, just leave it alone for now. We were not harmed. You are home. We shall be safe now."

"I am going to talk to the army commander," I said. "I understand a new commanding officer has been brought in. This will give me an excuse to introduce myself and see what kind of fellow is in charge of the troops here."

"Now, what news do you have from Edinburgh?" Margaret asked. I think she was trying to distract me from going out. "I know you must have news to share."

"Ay. The opportunity arose and I made inquiries regarding the Covenanters who had been banished to the islands. I was able to learn that some of them, such as tailors, had been assigned tasks according to their skills instead of labouring in the broiling sun in the sugar cane fields. I did not learn anything specifically about Montgomery, but what I heard makes me hopeful that his situation is not as difficult as we feared."

"We must get word to his wife," Margaret said.

I laughed. "I knew you would say that."

"Hello, Father," a lovely young voice called to me. I turned to see Fiona running down the stairs. I hurried to meet her in the foyer. I picked her up and swung her around in my joy to see that she really was not physically harmed from the events of the past night.

"I am so glad to see you," I said as I set her feet back down on the stone floor. We steadied each other as the room continued to spin around us for a few moments. "Your mother has told me what happened while I was away. I am sorry I was not here to deal with your Mr. Campbell."

"Mother and I are fine. It was frightening at the time, but we are safe with you home now. And, Father, he is not 'my Mr. Campbell.'"

"Your mother said you recognized his voice. Can you tell me what he said?" I asked.

"Ay. The words were chilling." She quoted him just as Margaret had. "He sounded drunk, but I believe he meant every word of it."

"Those are the words your mother understood him to say. Interesting. Those are the exact words the soldier said to Mrs. Montgomery as he took her husband away from his shop that day."

"That proves he is the one who attacked Mr. Montgomery," Margaret said. "He was not just claiming he did it."

"It does not prove it," I said, "but it certainly strengthens the case against him – the coward. He thinks he is a man, but no true man sets out in the darkness to frighten women."

"You will not do anything to bring more trouble upon us, will you, Father?" Fiona asked.

"I have to report this to the company commander," I said. "Campbell cannae get away with this. It is a terrible position your Robert Campbell has put me in."

"He is not my Robert Campbell, Father. Please stop calling him that," Fiona said, and then she ran upstairs in tears.

I left Margaret to comfort Fiona, and I went to the army encampment. I met the new commander and was pleasantly surprised to find that he was an old army friend of mine, William Ross. He listened intently to my story as his aide-de-camp took copious notes. William assured me that this time Robert Campbell would be punished severely.

Just two weeks later, William sent word to me that Campbell was in the stockade in Glasgow. My family and I could finally travel the streets in safety and sleep peacefully at night, but Margaret made sure I did not forget Alexander Montgomery.

The flow of information was slow to cross the Atlantic, so answers to questions did not come quickly enough for Mrs. Montgomery. By the time winter set in, she had completely lost her health. My informant told me that her children were looking after her more than she was tending to them by the end of 1687.

I sent word to her just before Christmas that some of the tailors were being allowed to use their old skills in Barbados and I was hopeful that her husband was one of them. That was all I knew, and I told my informant to make sure Mrs. Montgomery understood that any information I got was six months old or more by the time it reached me. I was glad to be able to send her some encouraging news for

Christmas. She had worried about her husband working out in the heat of the tropical islands, so I was glad to be able to ease her fears somewhat.

***

The year 1688 was a turning point in Scottish history. Not so many years have passed between that time and the present, but as I write in 1703, I believe the events of 1688 gave Scotland the stability it needed for a lasting peace and religious freedom for her people. The last well-known Covenanter to be martyred, James Renwick, was put to death in February of that year in Edinburgh.

Once the Revolution started, everything happened fairly rapidly. It was in 1688 that King James was dethroned for breaking the Constitution. More specifically, he had failed to take the Coronation Oath. His demise made it possible for his daughter, Mary, and her husband, William, Prince of Orange, to jointly reign over England and Scotland. With William and Mary on the throne, the Church of Scotland was re-established.

I concluded then that Alexander Montgomery could safely return to Scotland. I made the necessary arrangements through my informants and the associates I had in the sugar cane business. When I knew the details had all been worked out, I told Margaret. She, of course, said we had to go immediately and tell Mrs. Montgomery. We called on her that very day and she was overjoyed at the news of her husband's imminent homecoming.

The next several months seemed to drag on as we anticipated Montgomery's return. He at last came home to Solway. His former landlord was happy to have him back and let him move back into his former shop and home. Mrs. Montgomery never regained her pre-1685 health, but her condition did improve after her husband's return.

Montgomery spoke only sparingly, to me at least, about his time in Barbados. He had spent the first year or so labouring in the sugar cane fields. The climate and tropical diseases nearly killed him and the work itself left his hands scarred from the many cuts and injuries sustained in the fields. He said he often wondered if he would have survived another year in the fields. He believed his being allowed to do tailoring the remainder of his captivity probably saved his life.

Though some one hundred men sailed from Leith on the ship with Montgomery in 1685, to his knowledge, only thirty-three were still living when he left the island to come home in 1688. In truth, he left Scotland a braw man of some forty-five years of age, but he returned just three years later giving the appearance of a man of sixty-five, if a day.

We all experienced a very trying time during "The Killing Time" – even those of us who were not persecuted. It was a time of self-examination for me. If it had not been for "The Killing Time" and, specifically, what happened to Alexander Montgomery, I maybe would have gone to my grave not knowing what I would do when morally tested. It is not easy for me to admit it, but I failed that test. I am proud that I eventually helped Montgomery and his wife and children and had a hand in making it possible for him to come home, but I shall forever have to live with the fact that I stood idly by when he was arrested and shipped to Barbados.

For those of you in future generations who might read this, I hope you will learn something from this story. If you have the privilege of living in a time of peace and freedom of religion, you owe a great debt to people like Alexander Montgomery who gave so much. If the authorities ever come after your neighbour because of his religion, do not turn your head and pretend it does not affect you. Remember – if they can come after your neighbour, they can also come after you.

And in case you are wondering why Mr. Montgomery's shears are still at Lochar Castle, I told him he could have them back or I would gladly buy a new pair of shears for him. He hesitated for a minute and then said, "If it is all the same to you, sir, I would prefer a new pair."

In appreciation for the new shears and all that Margaret and I had done for his family, he offered to make all the clothes my family needed as long as he lived. I told him that was not necessary – that I was just glad to have my tailor back and to see him reunited with his family. Having a happy ending to the story was all the repayment I needed.

Respectfully yours,
Sir Iain Douglas

Another Note from the Author:

Being raised in the Presbyterian Church, I was embarrassed that I did not learn about the Covenanters until I was an adult. If not for a trip to Scotland, it is possible that I never would have known about that important piece of Presbyterian history.

All the characters in this story are fictional; however, the events are based in fact. The tailor's shears are not documented, but are an example of an item that could have been used as a weapon against a Covenanting tailor in the late 1600s in Scotland.

Just as today the monarch was the head of the Church of England in the 1600s. The Covenanters refused to recognize the King as head of the Church because they firmly believed – just as Presbyterians believe today – that Jesus Christ is head of the Church.

Covenanters were brutally persecuted by the government. The "boot" was used. Two women were indeed drowned at Wigton in the rising tide while being tied to poles. Presbyterian ministers were banished from their pulpits. They held conventicles (secret worship services) wherever they could. I learned this was true in Campbeltown, Scotland where my Morrison ancestors lived in the 1600s and early 1700s, so this bit of Scottish history took on personal importance to me.

I could not begin to give the complete history of the Covenanters in this short story. A short story, being fiction, is not the place for such a deep dive into history. If this story has piqued your interest in the topic, please do your own research. One extraordinary resource, which was first published in 1905 and is now in the public domain, is *The Blue Flag: Or the Covenanters Who Contended for Christ's Crown and*

Covenant, by Robert Pollok Kerr. It can be read online and copies are available from online booksellers if you want your own copy.

YOU COULDN'T HELP BUT LIKE BOB

Tappahannock, Virginia

1712

You couldn't help but like Bob. Unless he owed you money. Unless you were a Justice of the Peace in Essex County, Virginia in the early 1700s.

Even so, you just couldn't help but like Bob.

To say Bob was irritating would be an understatement, but you couldn't stay mad at him for long. Unless he owed you money or tobacco. Unless you were a Justice of the Peace, tired of seeing him dragged into your court room.

Fresh off the ship from Ireland early in 1712, Bob was eager to establish himself as a tobacco planter. He figured that was not only the economically prudent thing to do but also the best way to land himself a wife.

Being single and just shy of twenty-four years old, he figured he had a good fifteen or more years ahead of him. He was ready to see what this

New World in Virginia had to offer. The way he saw it, he had nothing to lose.

He had paid his way across the Atlantic by doing anything and everything that needed doing on the ship. Little did he know when he signed on that he would be seasick from start to finish. He had never seen an ocean worthy vessel before the day he arrived at the quay to seek passage. He had never even seen the ocean.

Off that stinking ship he never wanted to see again, he was still trying to walk again on solid ground coming up Queen Street in Tappahannock. Sweat trickled into his eyes as he was confronted with a heat and heaviness in the air that he had never experienced back home. He wondered if he was sick with some dread disease he had picked up on the ship, or was it this unbearably hot and humid in Virginia?

Even without the benefit of a looking glass, Bob knew he looked ragged. He tucked his unruly hair behind his ears. The ribbon he used to tie his hair back in a queue was long gone. His hat had blown off last week and was, no doubt, still bobbing along somewhere in the Atlantic Ocean. All his clothes except the pants and shirt he had on had been stolen.

Bob had ambition on his side, though, and was excited to be off that God-forsaken ship and in America where everyone was welcome and the cobblestone streets were lined with opportunities for wealth. You just had to want it bad enough, and Bob did.

He was lost in his newfound physical misery and mental euphoria when he bumped into a man as he approached what he later learned was called Church Street. The man sized up Bob as a clumsy pickpocket and started hurling insults at him.

"You good for nothing scoundrel! A thief! A pickpocket! A drunk!"

Not one to go looking for a fight, Bob never walked away from one. If a man wanted to pick a fight with him, Bob was happy to oblige.

"I'm not a drunk. In fact, I'm not any of those things, and I don't appreciate being called names."

Finding his footing, Bob hauled off and slugged the man in the jaw. A few minutes later, Bob found himself in jail. He learned from the other inmates that misbehavior was frowned upon in the wee village, and almost anything qualified as misbehavior.

The Justice of the Peace glared down at Bob a few days later, his white wig a bit awry. A large wart on his nose kept his spectacles from sliding off his face. Bob had several minutes to study the Justice while His Honor read the charges against him. From the man's ruddy complexion, Bob surmised the Justice was fond of drink. He tucked that information away in case he could benefit from it later.

Bob suppressed a yawn and tried to stand tall and straight. He noticed the other men in the court room were dressed a good deal better than he and they all bore looks of disdain on their faces. He had a hunch fitting into the local society was going to be more difficult than he had anticipated.

The Justice informed Bob that he did not appreciate trouble makers, especially new arrivals from Ireland. He did not want the town to get a bad reputation, so he was going to do everything in his power to teach Bob a lesson he would not soon forget.

Bob braced himself for whatever punishment lay ahead. Visions of being confined in a pillory for a few hours danced in his mind. He figured he could withstand that, even with pious church members yelling insults at him. How bad could it be?

But charged with fighting and disturbing the peace, Bob was ordered to pay the court fifty pounds of tobo. Bob was reluctant to ask what that was, but he had a hunch that was what the locals called tobacco. New World. New vocabulary.

What Bob knew about tobacco could slip through the eye of a needle with plenty of room left over for all he knew about living in a hot, humid climate. What he lacked in knowledge, though, he more than made up for in charm, self-confidence, and enthusiasm.

Bob secured a bed to sleep in that night at a tavern. Sleeping in a bed with two other dirty strangers was not what he thought America would be like, but he made the best of it and tried to go to sleep before the other two started snoring. It was Friday, and he decided that night to set out the next day to learn all he could about tobacco and how he could get his hands on fifty pounds of it.

His face and neck had blistered after his hat blew off on the Atlantic. Having his skin turn red, blister, and peel off in pieces the size of his hand was a new experience for Bob. *Is this what I have to look forward to in this New World? I need to get a hat and soon. It will also serve to keep my hair under control until I can purchase a ribbon to tie it back with.*

The dusty streets were busy with women and their children doing their shopping the next day. It didn't take long for Bob to figure out that he was out of place among them, so he purchased a ribbon and a hat, and wandered down to the banks of the Rappahannock River in hopes of finding some men to talk to.

The very sight of the ship and fishy smell that hung in the breeze coming off the river made his stomach churn, but it was there that he found the kind of activity he wanted. This was a new day and he soon learned a new word. Here, it was a wharf, not a quay. The sooner he learned things like this, the sooner he would fit in and be accepted, or so he thought.

In conversation with the men hanging out at the wharf, he learned about the price and availability of land and the growing season. He inquired about getting a job working on a tobacco plantation and got several good leads to follow up on the following week.

Bob left the wharf feeling encouraged about his financial prospects and headed back into the village. There, he noticed an attractive woman of about his age or a little younger. She wasn't wearing a wedding band and she wasn't surrounded by a herd of children, so he thought she might be someone he would like to spend some time with.

What he could see of her hair from around her bonnet was a lovely amber. Perhaps she, too, was from Ireland. He would know immediately from her accent if she would talk to him.

Glad he had that new hat hiding his oily hair and some of his blistered face, he ambled up to her as she was looking at some green vegetable he'd never seen before. Her eyes were emerald like the hillsides back home. The very vision of her made tears sting his eyes.

"Do you need help carrying your purchases?" he asked.

Startled, she took a step back from him. "I don't normally accept help from a stranger." There was a hint of Irish in her words and demeanor.

Bob removed his hat to show respect but immediately remembered how he must look. He swallowed hard as sweat rolled down his face. "I mean you no harm. Can you at least tell me what vegetable you're buying? I've never seen it before."

"Yes, it's okra. Slave ships from Africa bring it."

"Do I hear a bit of an Irish accent in your voice?"

"No, I was born here. My parents are Irish."

"Born here? I can't imagine! Do you and your parents live here in the village or does your father own a plantation?"

The young woman hesitated and seemed nervous.

"I'm sorry," Bob said. "I've asked a personal question. Forgive me."

"You seem interested in more than the name of okra."

"Pardon me. I must seem rude. My name is Bob Dooling."

"I'm Ann. Mrs. Ann Coffey."

It was as if all the air had been sucked out of Bob's lungs. His faced burned more from embarrassment than his sunburn. "You aren't wearing a wedding band. I assumed –"

"No need for apologies, Mr. Dooling. My husband is deceased. I maintain my own home. My father does own a plantation."

"I just arrived a few days ago, and I want to learn all about tobacco. Do you think I might be able to work for your father?

"He might be amenable to such an arrangement. Perhaps I can introduce you to him at church tomorrow."

Church. Bob hadn't planned to go to church.

Ann waited for Bob to react. She, no doubt, expected enthusiasm. While he remained silent, she pointed and indicated that the church was just up the way and that was why it was called Church Street.

It took Bob a few seconds to find his voice. "I'll be there. I'll see you, I mean, I'll see your father there. I'm much obliged."

They parted ways, and Bob could not believe his good fortune. In Virginia less than a week, he had already met the woman of his dreams and had good prospects for a job on a plantation.

That night, Bob lay in bed thinking about all that had happened that day. He was confident that Mrs. Coffey's father would hire him, but having a job did not give him the fifty pounds of tobo he needed to get the Justice of the Peace off his back. Bob concluded the best way to come by an amount of tobacco fast was to win some in a card game. First things first, though, he had to go to church in the morning and make a good impression. The card game would have to wait.

Bob slipped into the church at the last minute and took a seat at the back of the sanctuary. The pew was hard and narrow. After very little sleep the night before and not knowing the order of things in the Church of England, he had trouble sitting still.

From where he sat, Bob recognized the back of Mrs. Coffey's beautiful head. He assumed the children sitting alongside her were younger brothers and sisters and the man and woman on the other side of the children must be her parents.

When the service finally ended, Bob rushed outside and found a shade tree to stand under. He watched the church door and his heart leaped into his throat when he saw Mrs. Coffey. She was so lovely and he could not help but notice how attentive she was to her younger siblings. What a sweet older sister she was, and what a fine mother she'd make someday.

The introductions went well, and Bob found Mrs. Coffey's father, Thomas Powell, easy to talk to. He was open to Bob visiting him the next morning and said he would give Bob a tour of his tobacco fields.

Bob was relieved that neither Mrs. Coffey nor her parents invited him to join them for dinner. After all, he had set his mind on a game of cards that afternoon. He fancied himself being a right smart card player and thought he could probably teach the residents of Tappahannock a thing or two about gambling.

Not being at all familiar with the local laws and not being an overly religious man, Bob found three fellows looking to pass a Sunday afternoon in a friendly game of cards. An expert at hiding his true feelings, he chuckled to himself and decided to have a little fun.

The three fellows looked like they were even more down on their luck than he was, so Bob hemmed and hawed, and claimed he really did not know much about cards. The men exchanged glances. He had them right where he wanted them.

"So you're no good at cards?" one of the men asked.

"No, not very good. I've hardly had any experience playing cards."

"I don't believe I've seen you before," one of the other men said.

"I just arrived a couple of days ago from Ireland."

The men laughed. "Never would've guessed it from your accent," one of them said.

Bob was immediately reminded that he was in a new country. He would need to work harder at fitting in.

"So you haven't learned how to play much yet?" the talker in the bunch asked.

"No, I've been so busy getting settled in, learning the lay of the land, I haven't had time to play at all. Maybe you fellows could teach me how you play cards in Virginia."

Their eyes brightened, just as Bob expected.

"Yes, we can teach you, can't we?" the talker said as he looked around at the other two men.

"I wouldn't want to put you out," Bob said. "It might be a waste of your time to try to play with someone like me. Maybe I could just watch you play and learn that way."

The men exchanged knowing looks and did not hide their delight. Bob could practically see the wheels turning in their heads. "No, pull up a shipping crate and have a seat. We'll help you along."

Bob tried his best to act dumb, but he was so good at card games it was difficult for him not to win. He asked questions that only a novice would need to ask. He watched the men's faces to gauge if he was fooling them. It looked to him as if things were going his way. He would wait until the last minute to show his hand.

The man who did most of the talking apologized and said he needed to excuse himself for a minute. Bob and the other two men agreed to pause the game and not cheat in his absence. As he stood to leave, the man placed his cards face down on the table with promises all around that no one would look at his cards while he was gone.

As the minutes ticked by, Bob grew antsy, but he noticed that his two companions seemed unperturbed that their friend had been gone an extraordinary amount of time to answer nature's call.

Bob was beginning to think they had all been tricked when the man returned. He apologized for taking so long, picked up his hand of cards, and asked whose turn it was.

It was agreed that it was indeed Bob's turn. Bob drew a card, took a deep breath, and opened his mouth to announce that he thought he had gotten lucky, but just then the sheriff arrived.

Calling each of the three men by first name, he thanked them for their assistance and promptly arrested Bob for playing cards on the Sabbath.

Bob spent the next three nights in jail before the Justice of the Peace (the one already acquainted with him) ordered him to pay the parish church fifty pounds of tobo.

What a predicament he was in now! He not only was deeper in debt, he had missed his meeting with the man he hoped would be his employer and future father-in-law.

The only thing to do, if he had any chance of getting better acquainted with Widow Coffey, was to visit Mr. Powell, confess his guilt, and hope the man would be willing in his Church of England heart to overlook the error of Bob's ways.

He longed to think of Mrs. Coffey as "Ann" instead of "Mrs. Coffey" or "Widow Coffey." She was far too young and attractive for those titles. Emboldened with thoughts of "Ann," Bob made his way to Mr. Powell's home.

After more than a few awkward minutes of difficult conversation interspersed with long periods of silence, Mr. Powell said something to the effect that everyone should be allowed a few lapses in judgment when they are in a new country with different laws and expectations.

With that, Mr. Powell showed Bob around his tobacco fields and tobacco barns, asked Bob what his motivations were for wanting to learn about the crop, asked Bob what family he had. Somewhere along the way, Mr. Powell mentioned how fond he was of Ann's children.

Bob hoped Mr. Powell had not seen his reaction to this news, which likely showed on his face.

Bob had much to think about on his way back into Tappahannock. The main thing he needed to accept was that Ann had children. Not just one or two children. She had six children and was obviously older than she appeared.

There was no turning back now. Bob was smitten. He had his sights on Ann and now had all the incentive he needed to be a successful planter and win her heart and devotion. If that meant providing for her six children, so be it.

In the coming months, Bob proved himself to be a hard worker. As ordered by the Justice of the Peace, he paid the church a total of 100 pounds of tobacco. He cleaned himself up, dressed in new clothes, and secured shelter in a barn loft on the Powells' plantation.

Bob attended church every Sunday so he could have an opportunity to talk to Ann. They were soon on a first-name basis with one another and he almost always was invited to follow her and her children home after the worship service for dinner.

Not only was Ann a good mother, she was an excellent cook and ruined Bob for the other meals he had during the week. He discovered that he liked fried okra.

Bob made it a habit to find her doing her weekly shopping in town on Saturdays, usually arriving in time to escort her and carry her purchases to her home. They soon had Mr. Powell's blessing, and Ann agreed to be Bob's wife.

One day, Bob met his old friend the Justice of the Peace on the street. Bob wanted the judge to know that he had gotten his life under control and was now happily married. The Justice made the mistake of making a snide comment about the character of any woman who would marry the likes of Bob.

Bob had not had an occasion to be in a fight in a long time, but he could not walk away from one when the opportunity arose. He spent the next week in jail for "abusing" a Justice of the Peace.

When Bob returned home, he asked Ann how she ever fell in love with him.

"I suppose I just couldn't help but like you and, before I knew it, I loved you."

Author's Note:

Robert Dooling and Ann Powell Coffey Dooling were my fifth-great-grandparents. It is thought Robert immigrated from Ireland. I don't know whether he was known as Robert or as Bob, but calling him Bob suited the fictional story I wanted to write about him. Ann's ancestry goes back to the 17th century in coastal Virginia and was actually British. The 1719 court records my sister and I found for Robert Dooling inspired the story. I took literary license with the year, the fines, and his three-day jail sentence. I know nothing of his personality, but the fact that he was in and out of trouble with the law in Colonial Virginia, influenced the way I wrote the short story. Since there was no separation of church and state in Colonial Virginia, fines imposed in the courts were often ordered to be paid to the Church of England or Anglican Church.

Here are some of the facts about Robert Dooling: Robert was arrested in Essex County, Virginia, in June 1719 on a suit brought by Thomas Cooper Dickenson. When Robert failed to appear in court in June and again in August 1719 to answer to Mr. Dickenson's suit, he was fined 200 pounds of "Tobo with one attorneys fee & costs."

Robert was charged with playing cards on the Sabbath and for "contemptuously abusing" two Justices of the Peace in Essex County, Virginia in November 1719. He was fined "one pound curnt money to His Maty King George to ye use of ye Governor for his sd abuse & also five Shill[ings] Curnt money to ye sd use according to Law for his sd breach of ye Sabbath & It's likewise ordered that he be & remain in ye Custody of ye Sheriff till he pay both aforesd fines with cost." I'm not sure how he was supposed to come up with the money while being held in jail.

Robert was taken into custody along with three other men (including Thomas Cooper Dickenson, mentioned above) for not showing up for court on February 22, 1720, in Essex County, Virginia, apparently due to a debt he owed W.M. Winston. In court on February 23, 1720, it was noted that Robert had been arrested. The case was continued on June 20, 1721. On July 18, 1721, Robert failed to appear in court for this case and was fined 400 pounds of tobacco with an attorney's fees and costs.

On March 22, 1720, Robert was fined 58 pounds of tobacco in a case filed by Thomas Waring, but the transcribed court proceedings did not give details of the case.

On January 21, 1723, Robert failed to appear for court. He and his security, Stephen Chenault, were fined 730 pounds of "Sweet scented Tobo" to be paid to the plaintiff, Anthony Gouldson.

The following day, Robert failed to appear for court to answer the suit of Edward Murrain and Martha, his wife, in a slander case. On April 21, 1724, Robert was ordered to pay Elizabeth Wilson "for one days attendance as an Evidence at ye suit of Edwd. Murrain etc." At that same court date, Mr. Murrain was ordered to pay one of his witnesses for one day's attendance in court and another witness for three days' attendance at court. In court on April 21, 1724, a jury of 12 men was impaneled to hear the case. After deliberating for "a short time" the jury found Robert guilty. On May 20, 1724, Robert was ordered to pay Mr. and Mrs. Murrain "Thirty shillings Sterl. damaged & three hundred pounds of tobo for costs of suit."

Robert was ordered to pay James Booth and Thomas Davis 600 pounds "of tobo in Cask" in a debt case in 1724.

Through all these years or court cases, Salvator Muscoe continued to be a Justice of the Peace, so one can imagine how weary he became of seeing Robert Dooling (or not seeing Robert Dooling!) in court so often. Two Justices were present for each court held.

John Bell accused Robert Dooling with trespassing and assault in 1727 in Essex County.

Robert Dooling died in Essex County, Virginia, in 1735, and Ann Dooling died there in 1744.

So far, Robert Dooling is the most colorful character on my family tree.

TO RUN OR NOT TO RUN

The Waxhaws, South Carolina
Mid-1700s

George and his father Jatta, bounced around in the back of Mr. Mc-Corkle's wagon. George and Jatta were slaves that Mr. McCorkle had acquired when their owner in Camden, South Carolina could not pay Mr. McCorkle the money he owed him.

At 10 years old, George was tall for his age. He removed his hat and fanned his face. Sweat trickled down his back in the broiling July sun.

"Where we going?" George asked.

"Let's just whisper to each other. Can't have the new master hearing us."

"Sorry," George whispered.

"Mr. McCorkle said a place called The Waxhaws," Jatta whispered. "From where the sun sits, it must be west of where we've been."

"What you think of our new master?"

"Don't rightly know yet. Wait and see. Behave and you ought to be all right."

"Yes, Papa."

The farther they went, the worse the road got. Dust stirred up by the team of horses and wagon wheels rose up and at times George coughed. Dust and sweat stung his eyes.

"You crying?" Jatta whispered.

"No, just trying to wipe the sweat and dust out of my eyes," George whispered.

The road being no more than a rutted path, George held onto the side of the wagon with all his might. "What if a wheel falls off, Papa?"

"I reckon I'll have to put it back on. You worry too much. Stop borrowing trouble."

George sensed his father was tiring of his questions, so he shut his eyes tight and tried to turn off his mind. But the harder he tried not to think, the more questions flooded his head. The ones that kept crowding out all the others were ones he knew not to ask because he was afraid his papa did not know the answers. *When will we see Mama again? When are we going to be free?*

George thought about the stories his papa had told him about how it was to be free back in Africa – a place called Senegal. Ships came from places unknown and brought captives across the great water to Charles Town.

Jatta did not like talking about his time on the ship. Maybe later, when George was older. Jatta had been all over. The slave market in Charles Town, later the one in North Carolina near Cross Creek. That is where he was sold and taken to Camden.

George was born in Camden and had never set foot off the planta-tion until this morning. After a tearful goodbye to his ailing mother, everything else blurred in his head. So many things he had never seen or heard before. Jatta pleading with Mr. McCorkle to take George, too. He had never seen his papa cry until this morning. First, when he kissed his dying wife goodbye, and second, when Mr. McCorkle said he just wanted Jatta. Said a scrawny little boy was no use to him.

"Please, Mr. McCorkle," Jatta had said with rivers of tears running off his cheeks and falling to the ground. It was the first time George had seen his papa on his knees begging, and it ripped something apart in his chest. George knew in a moment that he would never see his papa the same way ever again. That vision of his papa was seared on his eyes and he knew in his heart he would never be able to unsee it.

"You sure you aren't crying?" Jatta whispered.

George turned his face away from his papa. He swiped at his eyes and then looked at Jatta. "Yes, a little."

"Missing your mama?"

"Yeah. That's it."

Jatta put his arm around George's shoulders. They rode in silence for miles and miles. Safe and leaning into his papa, George fell asleep.

***

The moon was high in the sky that night when they arrived at the McCorkle farm. Jatta nudged George awake. He woke with a start. Jatta held him tight so he would not fall. The wagon eased down a lane between a barn and open pasture land and came to a halt at a small but sturdy-looking log cabin.

Even in the moonlight, George saw a better built and maintained cabin than the one he had been born and raised in back in Camden. He and Jatta jumped down from the wagon. As George ran around to catch up with Mr. McCorkle at the cabin door, Jatta stretched and reached to rub his lower back.

The door squeaked open. George followed Mr. McCorkle into the cabin by the light from his master's lantern. By the time Jatta caught up with them, Mr. McCorkle had taken a wheat straw from the fireplace mantle and lit the lantern sitting on the hearth. The room had the musty smell of a place that had not been used in a while.

With, "I'll meet you at the barn at first light," Mr. McCorkle left them to settle in.

George slowly turned all the way around. The room was small but tidy. A closed door beside the chimney caught his attention. "Where does that go?" he whispered.

"Master's gone," Jatta said. "We don't have to whisper now. Won't know where that door goes till we look." Jatta picked up the lantern and turned the wick up just a little to make more light, then he slowly opened the door by the hearth.

"Papa! Another room! I've never seen a slave cabin with two rooms!"

Three beds pretty much filled the space. There were wooden pegs on the wall for hanging clothes. George ran his hands over one peg after another. *We don't have any clothes but the ones we have on. We don't have anything. We don't even have Mama now. I hope Papa can't see I'm crying again.*

✳✳✳

"You'll need to prove your worth to Mr. McCorkle," Jatta said, several days later.

"So he'll let me stay with you?" George asked.

"I'm afraid so. Can you name the crops here?

"Wheat and Indian corn."

"Name the animals. You have to learn all about the animals."

"Pigs, milk cows, beef cattle, chickens. Is that all?

"You forgot one."

George closed his eyes. He hoped that would help him think.

"They're little, but there are lots of them," Jatta said.

"Bees! How could I forget the bees and the beescapes?"

"Keep your eyes and ears open all the time. It's important for you to remember everything you can. The more you know how to do, the more valuable you will be to Mr. McCorkle."

"So he'll let me stay."

"Yes, so he'll let you stay."

"I saw Mr. McCorkle's son today. I think he's about my age."

"Did he say anything?"

"No, we weren't close. I was getting a drink of water at the spring, and he was in the apple orchard."

"If you're ever close to each other, remember to let him speak first."

"What if he asks me a question?"

"Answer him."

No sooner had Jatta said that, there was a knock at the door. Jatta opened the door.

"I'm William McCorkle," the young white boy said.

George jumped up and peeped around his father to see the boy.

"My mother sent these clothes for George," William said. He held a stack of three neatly folded shirts. She said if they don't fit, he will grow into them."

"Much obliged," Jatta said, accepting the clothes. "George?"

"Much obliged," George said. Careful not to look the boy in the eye, he tried to memorize the boy's clothes and size. His hair was reddish and light. The best he could tell, his eyes were blue. Blue eyes made him uncomfortable. So did silence, but he did not know what else to say.

"Guess I'll see you around," William said. "What do you like to do for fun, George?

Moisture gathered in the palms of George's hands at the same time his mouth went dry as cotton. "I --. Let me think. I --."

"Marbles?" William asked.

"I don't know. I don't know that game."

"Maybe I can show you sometime."

"Much obliged," George said.

William turned to leave, then looked back at George and put his hand up in an almost wave. George waved back, but William had turned toward the big house.

***

George especially liked to sit in the cool grass under the apple trees in the spring of the year when there was a soft breeze, birds singing of their joy that winter was over, and gray squirrels all about digging up the last of the prior fall's hidden acorns.

His favorite times were when Mrs. McCorkle could be heard playing her harpsichord. Not allowed in the McCorkles' big two-story house, he wondered what the instrument that made such beautiful music looked like. With the parlor window open, the melodies wafted out to the orchard and sometimes lulled George to sleep.

William taught him to play marbles, and George gradually felt at ease around him. He sensed that his association with William made his father nervous, but he repeatedly told Jatta that he was careful what he said around the boy.

Months passed, seasons changed, and George grew more interested in his papa's earlier life in Africa. When Jatta told him about the stringed musical instrument he played before he was kidnapped by a neighboring tribe and put on a slave ship to Charles Town, George was fascinated.

"Can you make one?" George asked.

"I can. I'll need to ask Mr. McCorkle if we can have one of the biggest gourds drying out in the barn."

George grinned. "Can I help you make it?"

"You can watch and help me. That way, you'll know how to make one yourself."

In the evenings when their work was done and Jatta wasn't too tired, they worked on the instrument. Jatta showed George how to stretch calfskin over a gourd he had cut down the middle.

"Try to use calfskin when you make one of these," Jatta said. 'It's thin and smooth and makes a nice sound."

"What if I don't have a calfskin?

"Sheepskin or goatskin will do, but try to get a calfskin when a calf has died or been slaughtered. You'll be happier with a calfskin. You'll be able to tell a difference in the sound, and so will other people."

While Jatta worked on the instrument, George asked questions about life in Africa. Jatta talked about the village where he lived, crops they grew, the wild animals, his parents, and anything else George wanted to know. Everything except his time on the slave ship.

"Is it almost finished?" George asked.

"Just one more thing and it will be," Jatta said. For a special finishing touch, Jatta carved his name in the neck of the gourd and handed it to George. "Now, learn to play it."

George beamed! "What's it called?"

"Back in Africa, it was called an akonting. I hear tell it's called a banjo here."

George repeated the African word slowly after his papa, careful to say each syllable. Then he said, "Banjo is easier to say."

"Depends on what you grow up speaking. You can call it a banjo, but always remember its real name is akonting."

"I will, Papa."

From that day on, George and the banjo were inseparable. When he worked in a field, he propped it up against a tree at the edge of the woods. When he stopped to eat lunch, he ate quickly so he could practice playing the banjo for a few minutes. He marveled at how well his papa could play and Jatta's talent gave him a goal to aim for.

***

With the passing of several years and lots of practice, George could play as well as his papa. He asked Jatta if they could make another akonting so they could play together.

It was about that time that George noticed a change in his papa. Jatta was slower to move, was easily upset, and developed a deep and crackling cough. Although getting weaker, Jatta continued to work. He told George not to tell Mr. McCorkle that he was not feeling well.

One night Jatta's coughing during the night was worse than ever before. When he started to cough up blood, George ran out of the cabin and to the McCorkles' house. It was very late, and the house was dark. George beat on the back door and yelled for help.

After what seemed like forever to George, Mr. McCorkle yanked the door open. "What's wrong, George? It's the middle of the night!"

"It's Papa. He was coughing and there was lots of blood. He told me not to tell you he was sick, but I didn't know what to do!"

"I'll come," Mr. McCorkle said. "I need to put on britches and shoes. You go on back to the cabin. I'll be there directly."

George ran back to the cabin and through the open front door. Jatta lay face down on the floor. George turned him over. "Papa! Papa! Wake up! Mr. McCorkle's coming. He'll know what to do. Wake up, Papa! You've got to wake up!"

Mr. McCorkle rushed in carrying a lantern and jug of what George suspected was whiskey. "Jatta!" Mr. McCorkle stooped beside the man and shook his shoulders. There was no response.

Mr. McCorkle stood up. "George, I'm afraid your papa is dead."

George's mouth opened but no sound came out. Not a scream. Not even a whimper. He stared at his papa's lifeless body, sure Mr. McCorkle was wrong. Sure his papa would speak and sit up at any moment, George just looked into his face.

Mr. McCorkle put his hand on George's shoulder. George jumped in surprise, for Mr. McCorkle had never touched him before and now he was touching him like a papa touches his own child. "If you don't want to stay in the cabin tonight with your papa's body, you can sleep in the barn. I'll see to his burial tomorrow."

***

The next weeks and months were difficult. George ached for his father. Loneliness ate at him every waking moment, and sleep was hard to come by. His banjo even sounded mournful. Mrs. McCorkle's harpsichord sounded happy, but he did not want to hear it. He doubted he would ever be happy again. He tried to remember what happy felt like, but he could not quite grasp it.

One night as he lay in bed he thought about his mother and wondered if she was still alive. *Papa said she probably didn't live through the day we told her goodbye, but how did he know that? Maybe she got better. There's only one way to find out.*

George got out of bed, picked up his banjo, and started walking east toward Camden.

He walked all night. The rising sun assured him that he was heading toward Camden. As he walked, he imagined the route in his mind. *When I get close to town, I'll just keep doing like I'm doing now, staying close to the woods by the road and jump into the pine forest when I hear a horse or wagon coming. I won't go into town. I'll sneak around it through the woods and such till I get to the plantation where Mama is. She'll throw her arms around me and hug me like she can't let go. I'll be so happy to see her again! I have so much to tell her!*

Or maybe she isn't there anymore. Maybe Papa was right. Maybe she died that day. Or the next day. When she realized we weren't coming back, maybe she died because she was too sad to live. No! She must still be there. She has to be.

Although George's banjo weighed very little, the longer he walked, the heavier it got. He held it in one hand and switched to the other hand when he felt his muscles cramping. *Maybe I should have left it behind. Maybe I was stupid to bring it.* He considered putting it down. He stopped and bent over, but as soon as the banjo touched the dusty road a shiver ran through his body. He gripped the banjo and snatched it up. He held it to his chest and vowed he would never let anything happen to the instrument. *Papa made it with his own hands with the skill he brought from Africa. This isn't just a banjo or akonting. It's part of my family. It connects me to Papa and to when he was free. This banjo means freedom. This banjo and I will be free someday.*

"There he is!" George heard William McCorkle shout. He had gotten so lost in his thoughts that he forgot to listen for travelers.

George wanted to run but his legs felt like lead. He willed his feet to move, but they refused.

The McCorkles' wagon came to a halt beside George. "Where are you going?" Mr. McCorkle asked. His tone was kind.

"Back to my mama."

"That's not a good idea," Mr. McCorkle said. "Come on back with William and me. Get in the wagon." His tone was still kind, but George knew it was an order and not a question.

George did not move.

"Come on," William said. "I'll ride in the back with you."

George cut his eyes toward William, who was sitting with his father on the wagon seat.

"It'll be fun," William said.

"Fun?" George said. *Maybe for you.*

"Get in the wagon, George," Mr. McCorkle said. "Don't make this harder than it needs to be. We need to get on back. You have work to do."

William jumped down from the wagon and walked around to George. "You know you have no choice."

George's shoulders slumped. Every muscle in his body felt defeated. He glanced at William's face. *Blue eyes that had always known freedom and always would. I wonder what the world looks like through blue eyes.*

George climbed into the back of the wagon and clutched his banjo. William jumped into the wagon and sat beside George, their feet dangling off the back. Mr. McCorkle directed the horses and got the wagon turned around. Within minutes the sun was hot on George's back.

***

Mrs. McCorkle took pity on the 14-year-old George and persuaded her husband to let George have a bed in the kitchen house loft. George and William became as close as a white boy and a slave boy could be, but George had to call the younger white boy, "Mr. William" and both always knew their standing in relation to each other and their standing in the community. It was an unspoken understanding.

George worked hard, so if his papa was looking down on him, he would be proud. Mr. McCorkle seemed pleased with his work. Twelve-year-old William often worked side-by-side with George.

"Sometimes I almost forget you're a slave," William said one day. "Do you ever forget it?"

"Can't say I do," George said. He did not dare to say anymore. He did not say what he wished he could say. *How can I forget that your papa owns me. How can I forget that I can't come and go as I please? How can I forget I only have one name, just like a dog?*

George continued to work and act like nothing had happened between him and William. He appreciated the kindness shown by Mr. and Mrs. McCorkle and did not want to say or do anything to upset them.

Ten years passed and George still dreamed of someday being free. He always looked for Clarissa, a pretty free woman on Sundays at the Waxhaw Meeting House. He wondered how a dark-skinned woman was free. *Had she ever been a slave?* He wanted to ask William, but he was afraid he would get in trouble. *Clarissa sure is pretty. I wonder if she has noticed me. I wonder if she thinks she's better than me since I'm a slave. I wonder if she could tell me how to get free. I wonder what it would be like to just talk to her and hear her speak to me. How can I get a chance to talk to her?*

***

Mr. and Mrs. McCorkle both got sick and died just days apart. William inherited George and the farm. The two young men continued to work together, but George still lived in the slave cabin and "knew his place." George had high hopes that William would free him after his parents died, but William never even hinted at it.

William seemed to trust George completely. In fact, he hired out George to play his banjo for parties in the community and gave George a little bit of the money his banjo playing made.

George was sweet on Clarissa. He thought if he could save enough money, he could buy his freedom and then have a chance of winning her over. Clarissa did day work for William McCorkle, so she was a constant temptation for George.

As time went on, George got so obsessed with buying his freedom that he started skimming a few coins here and there when he took a crop to market or when William sent him to buy something. When William caught George in a lie about some money, their trust was shattered.

"I have a mind to sell you!" William shouted. "And don't think for a minute I won't." But William did not know that it was not the first time George had cheated him, so he did nothing except yell at the slave and, out of obligation, reported the incident to the church elders at Waxhaw Meeting House.

George was found guilty of stealing. His punishment was not being allowed to take communion until the Session said he proved that he had repented. There was a new wall between George and William. George could not see it, but it was there sure as if it had been made of stone. George no longer spoke to William unless spoken to. George knew he had to regain William's trust or he would be miserable and have no hope of ever being free.

"You've embarrassed me," William said. "No one in the McCorkle household – including slaves – has even been called before the church Session for any transgression. This is a stain on my reputation."

"Yes, sir, Mr. William. I understand that. I'm sorry. I wish I could undo what I did."

Several months passed, and William told George he was going to Salisbury. "I'll be gone for five days and you'd better be here when I get back. If you do anything out of the way while I'm gone, so help me I'll sell you so fast it'll make your head spin. Understand?"

"Yes, sir, Mr. William."

"Don't set foot off my property. Not to visit Clarissa. Not to pick a fight with Caesar over on the Thompson place. Not to play your banjo at a party. You understand?"

"Yes, sir, Mr. William. I sure do."

"I'm leaving at first light in the morning. I'll be back on Friday evening. You have plenty to do, so you won't have time to get in trouble."

"No, sir, Mr. William. That's right."

George walked to his cabin. He lay on the bed and stared at the cobwebs on the ceiling until darkness swallowed them. His mind whirled. He had two choices. He could stay or he could run.

If I stay, I have a roof over my head, plenty to eat, still get to see Clarissa once in a while, have a chance to win her over someday. On the other hand, I have no future if I stay. I'm only fooling myself. I'll never have Clarissa. I'll always be a slave. I've ruined what I had with Mr. William. Clarissa knows I stole from Mr. William, so she'll never want me.

If I run, I have a chance to get all the way to … all the way to where? All the way to that river called Ohio? There's a better chance I'll get caught. Then Mr. William will surely sell me. I could end up somewhere worse. Mr. William's never laid a hand on me. Lots of slaves aren't so lucky.

But it sure would be sweet to be free. Free to do as I please. I could work and buy my own farm. Find me a wife. Or I could send for Clarissa. She'd be proud of me then. But I'd always be looking over my shoulder, scared of being found out. Scared of being sold as a slave again.

Before George knew it, the rooster crowed under his window and it was getting light. *Time to get up and get to work in the field. With Mr. William gone, I'll have all day to think.*

George worked in the field for a couple of hours. He saw William leave on his horse without even lifting his hand or nodding his head to acknowledge George existed. The more George thought, the angrier he got.

I don't owe Mr. William anything. Why am I still here? All I need to do is keep going north and stay out of sight. The sun will tell me which way to go in the daytime and the drinking gourd in the sky will direct me at night. How hard can it be to get to the Ohio? Others have made it. If they can, so can I.

By the time George had talked himself into leaving, his feet had left the field and gone to his cabin to fetch his banjo.

Author's Note:

George is a character of my imagination, as are his parents, Mr. and Mrs. McCorkle, and William McCorkle. George came about as I was writing the first draft of my first historical novel, which is probably going to be the second novel in my Great Wagon Road Series. He will have a small role in the first novel in the series.

Some fictional characters grab a hold of you and refuse to let go. George is one of them. He has a good heart. He makes some poor decisions in his life, but he had to make his own way in this world in a society that sometimes saw him as just two-thirds of a person and sometimes did not see him as a person at all. To Mr. McCorkle, George was little more than a piece of property.

I was eager to introduce George to you in this collection of short stories. Now, you can look forward to getting better acquainted with him and William McCorkle in my Great Wagon Road historical novel series.

I chose to use the McCorkle surname because it is a name from the early history of the Waxhaws section of South Carolina, and that name and place are in my family history.

Making the Best of a Tragedy

Salisbury, North Carolina

1760-1781

Elizabeth Gillespie washed the last of the dirty dishes in the kitchen of the tavern she and her husband, Robert, owned in Salisbury. She cleaned as much by feel as by sight in the dim light provided by a single candle.

Her back ached as she hung her apron on a knob on the pantry wall. In a few short hours she would return to that pantry to prepare breakfast for the night's lone lodger and any new travelers who might happen by.

Being at the crossroads of the Great Wagon Road from Philadelphia and the Trading Path from Fort Henry, Virginia, into the lands of the Cherokee and Catawba, this Carolina backcountry village was always on the edge of excitement and boredom in late February 1760.

Elizabeth's lodger that night was a fur trader on his way to visit the Cherokee. Upon learning of his plans, she had done her best to dissuade him from continuing on his way.

"Have you not heard about the current threats from the Cherokee?" she asked him while serving him his supper. Against her better judgment, Elizabeth told him that her husband was in fact at Fort Dobbs now due to the troubles. *Was I foolish to tell him? Will he take advantage of my situation?*

The trader appeared to be overly confident as he told Elizabeth that the outpost for soldiers, traders, and colonial officials some thirty miles to the west was indeed his next stop.

Word had come that afternoon that the fort had been attacked by Cherokee, but the trader assured Elizabeth that her concerns were unfounded. After all, the French and Indian War to the north was winding down. More peaceful times were coming and her tavern just feet from the crossroads was perfectly situated to reap the benefits of the rush of Scottish and German settlers who were eager to leave Pennsylvania and settle on cheaper land in the wide-open spaces of North Carolina.

She was glad when the trader finally went upstairs to his room for the night. Her gut told her that Robert was in serious trouble and the trader had either misjudged the news or was trying to allay her fears.

The news from Fort Dobbs repeated in Elizabeth's head as she looked in on her sleeping children, Margaret and Bobby. She said a quick prayer for their safety and for Robert before going to her husband's desk to catch up on the day's bookkeeping.

The leather-bound ledger felt heavier than usual as Elizabeth took it from the shelf and tried to collect her thoughts. How many guests had she prepared breakfast for this morning? Had it just been a few hours ago? How many customers had come in for a noonday meal?

All the while, Elizabeth imagined Robert at the fort. The Gillespies and others had taken refuge there more than once when tensions were high. All those times had been false alarms. Threats of Cherokee attacks had never panned out until today.

She was a woman of great faith, but Elizabeth was practical. Perhaps her worst fears had been realized in today's attack at the fort. She closed her eyes and remembered the layout of the fort. It was up on a knoll which allowed lookouts in every direction.

Had Robert enjoyed the camaraderie of the other men over breakfast in the dining hall that morning, or had he been invited to dine in the commander's quarters? What was he doing when the Cherokees attacked? Was he at the ready with his musket in hand or were he and the others caught by surprise?

Elizabeth repeated The Lord's Prayer and several familiar Psalms in the quiet late evening moments, barely aware of the steady ticking of the mantle clock in the adjacent dining room. She was tempted to lay her head down on her folded arms there at Robert's desk and take a nap in the first still moments of the long day.

No sooner had she entertained those thoughts when she heard voices out on the street. It was not unusual for travelers to arrive late in the evening or even in the wee hours of the morning. *Please don't come here needing a room. I'm too tired to help anyone else tonight. Morning will be here before I'm ready. I must try to get some sleep.*

The voices grew louder. Elizabeth grabbed her candle and rushed into the dining room. She desperately wanted to hear Robert's voice, but as she strained to listen it was not his voice she heard.

The front door burst open. "Mrs. Gillespie! Come quick!"

"Robert!" she screamed as two men assisted her bloodied and beaten husband into the tavern. Bile rose in her throat. She couldn't breathe. There was so much blood, she could not tell where he was wounded.

She rushed to pull out a chair for the men to seat Robert in. The rag covering his head was dripping blood. She searched the eyes of the men holding her husband.

"It's bad, Mrs. Gillespie," one of the men said. "He was scalped."

Elizabeth felt as if she'd been punched in the stomach. For what seemed like a couple of minutes she could not breathe or speak. *Oh dear God! Oh dear God! Oh dear God, help us.*

***

Taking care of Robert was grueling as he suffered unspeakable pain. Elizabeth could scarcely bear the sight and smell of his horrible wound. Within a few days, the stench took her breath away as well as her appetite. She knew it would be impossible for him to recover, and she wondered why God had allowed him to survive the attack at all.

It broke Elizabeth's heart that Margaret and little Bobby did not recognize their father. They repeatedly asked her when their father was coming home and who that stinking man was who lay on a cot in the back room.

When she had a minute to spare, she wrote a short letter to her brother, James Maxwell, who was a physician in Pennsylvania. She told him about Robert's wounds, how she was caring for him the best she could, and asked for any advice he could offer. She sent James the letter even though she knew the slowness and irregularity of postal service meant she would not receive James' reply in time to benefit Robert.

After twenty-nine days, Robert mercifully died. Elizabeth felt nothing but relief that he was no longer in pain. She prayed that the image of his wound would eventually fade from her memory.

On the ride home from the burial at Thyatira Meeting House, Margaret and Bobby asked questions about their father. They finally understood that the sick man in the back room was their father and he had been severely hurt by some Cherokee Indians who were angry at white people for taking their land.

***

Years passed and Elizabeth made the best of the situation in which she found herself. She married William Steele in 1763 and the tavern took the name Steele's Tavern. The Steeles weathered the years of the French and Indian War even as the backcountry remained sparsely populated.

With the end of the War, a steady stream of German, Scottish, and Scots-Irish immigrants poured down the Great Wagon Road. Salisbury became a hub of activity. Some of the travelers settled in Rowan County, while others pushed south to Rocky River and even beyond to the Waxhaws.

One evening, discussion at one of the dining tables at the tavern focused on Rev. Alexander Craighead. "Craighead, down at Rocky River, is too vocal in his displeasure with the King," one of the men said.

Elizabeth continued to replenish their mugs of apple cider.

"He was forced out of Pennsylvania years ago for his statements against the King," one weary-looking traveler said. "Then, he and most of his congregation fled Windy Cove up in Virginia due to hostile Indians. He's going to find himself in trouble again if he's not careful. Telling the people not to register their deeds to get around paying for the stamps! Who does he think he is? He needs to stick to preaching the Gospel and leave politics to somebody else."

"He seems to have found the perfect place for his political views down at Rocky River and Sugar Creek," Elizabeth said. "As a licensed Minister of the Word and Gospel, Rev. Craighead has the Christian authority to conduct marriage ceremonies. Who is the King to say he doesn't?"

Conversation at the table stopped. Elizabeth looked at the stunned faces around the table. "You seem surprised that I have an opinion or even knowledge of the situation."

"Ladies are usually quiet when it comes to politics," a man at the table said.

Elizabeth firmly planted her empty fist on her hip. "Your smirks speak for themselves. You might be surprised what we ladies know and think!"

The men exchanged glances and suppressed chuckles. "I would love to stay and discuss these matters with you gentlemen, but I have work to do." Elizabeth turned on her heels and approached another table of dinner patrons.

"Silly woman!" Elizabeth heard one of the men utter as she walked away. She gritted her teeth and forced a smile. *If they only knew what I have had to see and do in my life! How many of them have successful businesses? How many of them have taken care of a scalping victim for a month?*

Elizabeth started to refill the mugs of the men at a nearby table while enjoying their conversation about the Stamp Act. "I trust you have found your meal to be satisfactory," she said, when there was a lull in the conversation. She gathered their empty pewter plates as the three roughly-clad men answered in the affirmative.

"Those gents you were just talking to have no idea who they're tangling with," one of the men said. He leaned back in his chair and let out a belly laugh. "If you didn't have to hold your tongue to protect your business, you could argue those fellas down. Hopefully, they are just passing through."

"I can take it as well as they can give it," Elizabeth said.

"Aye. I believe you can," another man at the table said.

Elizabeth thanked the men for their patronage and took their dishes to the kitchen.

***

Elizabeth was in the perfect position to stay informed about the mood of the citizens. She engaged in conversation with her patrons and keep her ears open to private conversations as she moved among the tables in her dining room. By the spring of 1771, farmers and other citizens were increasingly frustrated with the provincial government which was top heavy with the wealthy and the citizens in the eastern part of the state. Governor Tryon was furious over the growing Regulator Movement.

"How long are you going to keep that portrait of King George hanging on that wall?" Herman Husband asked one day as she filled his mug with cider.

"Until you Regulators get us out from under his thumb," she said.

"We're working on it," he said.

"I know. People are losing patience."

"No one is less patient than I am." With that, Mr. Husband slapped a coin on his table and left.

A few weeks later, on a warm May afternoon, a traveler burst into the tavern. "Have you heard what happened?" the man said. All conversation and dishes clatter in the room stopped.

"No. What are you talking about, "Elizabeth said.

"The lads down at Rocky River blew up the King's gun powder shipment!"

"Here! Here!" a chorus of enthusiastic cheers rose up.

"Quiet, everyone," Elizabeth said. "Let the man tell us what he knows."

People turned in their chairs and leaned in to listen. Others stood and came closer to the messenger.

"Lads from Rocky River sneaked up on three wagons of gun powder last night at Phifer's Muster Grounds. The powder was bound for Rowan and Alamance counties to put down the Regulators. They grabbed the teamsters, got them out of the way, and set fire to the powder. The explosion was heard for miles!"

They've done it now!" a voice in the room said. "This will lead to war. Mark my words."

"We're already at war, as far as I'm concerned," another man said.

***

War weary General Nathaneal Greene and Army doctor Joseph Read came to Steele's Tavern on February 2, 1781, for something to eat and a place to collect their thoughts on their way to Guilford County.

Eager to learn any details of the war that she could, Elizabeth attended to General Greene and Dr. Read's table as slowly as she dared without creating their suspicion that she was eavesdropping. General Greene was visibly concerned about what the loss of General Davidson the day before in the Battle of Cowan's Ford meant to the Americans' cause.

"We fought together at Brandywine and met up again in Charlotte-town last September," General Greene said. "I depended on Davidson. It's a personal and a military blow I did not need. I am fatigued, hungry, and penniless."

"I will bring your food directly, General Greene," Elizabeth said.

After delivering the General's and doctor's food to their table, Elizabeth retired to her bedroom for a few minutes. She paced back and forth. *What should I do? I have some coins hidden away. Dear God, what should I do?*

A few minutes later, Elizabeth approached General Greene. She reached under her apron and retrieved two small bags of gold and silver coins. Handing the bags to the General, she said, "Take these for you need them and I can do without them."

The General's countenance brightened immediately. Before leaving the tavern, General Greene paused and looked at the prints of King George and Queen Charlotte hanging on the wall over his dining table. He took down King George's portrait. Taking a piece of chalk from his pocket, Greene wrote the following on the wooden backing in the frame: "O, George, hide thy face and mourn."

He then hung the picture back on the wall, but with King George's likeness facing the wall.

Author's Note:

While I was doing research in preparation for writing an historical novel set along the Great Wagon Road in North Carolina, I learned about Elizabeth Maxwell Gillespie Steele. She was a fascinating woman. Her first husband was indeed scalped by Cherokee Indians at Fort Dobbs, and he survived for an excruciating 29 days.

Being a successful businesswoman in her own right, Elizabeth did not remain a widow very long. In 1763, she married William Steele and they continued to operate her establishment as Steele's Tavern.

A group of young men from Rocky River Presbyterian Meeting House in old Mecklenburg County blew up three wagons of the King's munitions at Phifer's Muster Grounds at present-day Concord, North Carolina on the night of May 2, 1771. They blackened their faces to disguise themselves and after Cabarrus County was formed out of Mecklenburg County in 1792, they became known as "The Cabarrus Black Boys." The governor declared them fugitives from the law and unsuccessfully hunted them.

Governor William Tryon declared the young men who blew up the gun powder shipment as fugitives. The Battle of Alamance effectively ended the Regulator Movement two weeks later. Trials were held for the leaders of the Regulators, including Herman Husband. I have no proof that Mr. Husband ever visited Elizabeth's tavern or had a conversation with her.

Elizabeth was dealt another personal blow when her husband died in 1773.

Tensions reached a breaking point in 1775 when the residents of Mecklenburg County, just south of Salisbury, declared themselves independent from the rule of King George. The Mecklenburg Declaration of Independence was signed in Charlotte on May 20, 1775. After the colonies' representatives signed a Declaration of Independence the following year, all-out war was inevitable.

General Greene and General Davidson both fought in the Battle of Brandywine in 1777.

By 1780, the backcountry of the Carolinas was in the thick of the action. After the Battle of Charlotte in September 1780, General Lord Cornwallis called the village "a hornet's nest." On the heels of the Battle of Kings Mountain, General William Davidson was killed in the Battle of Cowan's Ford on the Catawba River on February 1, 1781.

General Nathanael Greene and Army doctor Joseph Read dined at Steele's Tavern the following day.

The rest of the story is true. The portrait of King George still exists and is in a protected location.

FROM SCOTLAND TO AMERICA

Glossary, Scottish to American:

Aye – yes

Bonnie – pretty

Brae – hillside

Burn – creek or stream

Cannae – cannot

Croft – farm

Dinnae – do not

Ken – know

Lad – boy or young man

Lass – girl or young woman

Quay (pronounced "kee") – wharf

"The wee toon" – nickname for Campbeltown, Scotland

Toon – town

Wee – small

Campbeltown, Scotland, and Pennsylvania
1762

The Crimson Arrow sailed out of Campbeltown Loch on the Kintyre coast of Argyll in Scotland. It had made the trip before with a seasoned captain and crew, and always stopped for an hour or so in Ballycastle, Ireland to take on more passengers and cargo as it made its way to America.

Five of the passengers were traveling together on this sailing – John and his wife, Mary; John's brother, James, and his wife, Jennet; and James and John's youngest brother, Robert.

The brothers had made various trips across the North Channel to Ireland, but Mary and Jennet never had even been on a small boat. *The Crimson Arrow* was a grand sailing ship.

The young women held tight to their husbands as they stood at the ship's railing. Mary had more than a few butterflies in her stomach as she looked down on the quay. Gannets and other seabirds swooped down trying to steal a fisherman's morning catch.

Mary's mind raced as she stood high up on the ship's deck. From this vantage point, the fishermen and their crews and other workers on the quay almost looked like ants scurrying around. The gentle rocking of the vessel was unsettling at first, but Mary soon grew accustomed to it.

Her eyes tried to take in everything so she'd never forget what "the wee toon" looked like, what it smelled like, what the often-heavy sea air felt like. *Will we live near the sea in America? I cannae imagine living in a place where I cannae see the water.*

The ship creaked and moaned. It rocked as cargo was loaded on and settled in place. The captain pointed and shouted at the workers to make sure the weight was distributed.

Mary jumped at the clanging of the ship's bell announcing it was time to depart. Campbeltown was the only home she or any of her family had ever known. *Are we doing the right thing? Am I ready for this adventure? John and his brothers want to own land in America, but I dinnae ken how that is possible. How can a crofter own his own land? Is anything in America like it is here? What if we get there and do not have enough money to buy land. What will become of us?*

The ship slowly began to move, and Mary held her breath and silently prayed she would not be seasick. She looked to her left at the brae and the crofts where the family had lived. Crossibeg. Baraskomill. Every croft had a name. She would someday tell her children about those crofts.

Before she knew it, the ship was entering Kilbrannon Sound. Mary and the others watched in silence as they looked back on Campbeltown and Davaar Island in the sea loch until the ship turned out of the sound and into the North Channel. "The wee toon" soon became just a speck in the distance.

The three brothers' mother had grown up on a croft named Eden at Southend on the Mull of Kintyre, so they had spent some happy times at Eden visiting their grandparents. With Campbeltown out of sight, they started craning their necks and squinting in the sunlight to catch a glimpse of the house and rolling green hills of Eden.

The men commented to one another when it came in view and regaled the women with stories they had no doubt told before of times spent with their grandfather Hall there and how "on a clear day you can see Ireland."

Soon, Eden disappeared in the distance, and John told Mary and Jennet that one of the first sights they'd see of the Irish coast would be the cliffs of Fair Head.

But no description John or his brothers could offer would prepare Mary and Jennet for Fair Head, for the cliffs were taller than anything the women had ever seen other than Ben Gullion, the wee mountain that overlooked Campbeltown.

Rising straight out of the waters of the North Channel, the sight of Fair Head took Mary's breath away. All she could do was point, her mouth open but no words escaped.

"Would you look at that? Must be as tall as Ben Gullion!" Jennet exclaimed.

"Not that tall, but more than half," James said. Although James and his brothers had seen Fair Head before, they couldn't help but gawk.

"I always forget how massive Fair Head is," Robert said. "Something else we'll never see again," his tone changing from awed to somber.

In a few minutes, the ship approached the quay at Ballycastle. The passengers were urged to stay onboard. They were warned that if they disembarked, they'd risk being left behind when the ship left for America.

Mary and Jennet longed to get off the ship and see what the shops in the village had to offer, but they were afraid they would be late returning to *The Crimson Arrow*. They did not want their husbands going to America without them, so they stayed on the ship.

More passengers boarded the ship along with various goods being sent to America for trade. Linen and Irish lace were always in demand across the ocean and brought a pretty price.

The ship gently rocked as the wind picked up. The captain barked out orders for his workmen to hurry up. "I'm anxious to take advantage of this wind!" he shouted above the hubbub of people talking and laughing and cargo being loaded.

The ship was soon moving again. County Antrim would be the last land the passengers would see for weeks to come. As the coast of Ireland shrunk and disappeared in the sea mist a few minutes later,

Mary and Jennet gave each other looks of resolve. "What have we gotten ourselves into?" Jennet asked Mary.

Mary shook her head and Jennet's eyes said *I don't know.*

***

There was much comradery on the ship as old acquaintances were renewed and new friendships made. Early on, there was much excitement and joy as the passengers shared their hopes and dreams and stories they had heard of the wonders of the New World.

Boredom, crying babies, and seasickness soon replaced those early pleasantries. Days turned into weeks and weeks turned into months. Squalls threatened to rip the tall sails off the ship and topple it into the angry sea. Days later there would be little if any breeze and the sun beat down on the ship and its passengers.

Finally, the welcome shouts of, "Land ho!" roused the passengers to their feet. They scrambled up the ladders to the deck of the ship, the sun blinding them until their eyes adjusted. Land was indeed in sight. They had made it across the sea!

There were shouts, and tears, and hugs, and men slapping one another on the back. There were silent and whispered prayers of thanks being offered to God for their safe arrival to the mouth of the Delaware River and ultimately, the port of Philadelphia.

Seagulls dived in all directions, seeing what morsels could be found as the latest ship from Scotland arrived and was unloaded of its wares. Bundles of Irish linen and lace came off the ship and into the waiting arms of merchants, but the ship mainly carried people and what little they brought with them. The ship's mission was to take timber back across the ocean. Having paying passengers coming west was a bonus.

Mary and Jennet carried what they could and staggered down the gangplank. Although the ship was fairly stable now, it still swayed a bit.

"Do you ladies need assistance?" a man asked.

"No, thank you," Mary said. "Our husbands are coming off the ship to meet us here at the quay."

"Very good," the man said. "By the way, it's called a wharf in America."

"I see," Mary said. She turned to Jennet. "Our first American word."

Mary squinted in the sun and tugged at the bill of her bonnet to give her face some relief from the heat. She fanned with her hand. "When John started trying to convince me to go to America, one of his strongest arguments was, 'It'll be warm there. I know how much you hate the cold.'"

Philadelphia went well beyond "warm." Mary had never been so hot in all her life. She turned to Jennet. There was a bond between the two that surpassed words. Their eyes and facial expressions communicated in a second what others would need several minutes to say with words.

Jennet nodded and wiped her brow with her handkerchief. "Aye," she said. "James said it would be warm here, but I didn't expect this!"

"I don't ken whether to laugh or cry," Mary said.

"In truth I dinnae care how hot it is," Jennet said. "I'm just glad to be off that ship."

The two young women still felt unsteady on their feet from nearly four months of living in the hull of that ship. They could not seem to stop swaying to and fro, so they held onto each other while they waited for their husbands and their unmarried brother-in-law, Robert, to catch up with them with their heavier items.

"There they come," Mary said, pointing toward the gangway. "It's funny how everyone walks off the ship like they're drunk."

"Aye, just like you and I did," Jennet said.

The women stood and waved to get their husbands' attention so they could find them in all the confusion and activity at the wharf. The men carried trunks that held all their worldly possessions.

"Looks like you have enjoyed a wee dram or two since we last saw you," Jennet teased Robert. She demonstrated how he was walking unsteadily in an exaggerated way.

"Oh, aye, that's what I was doing," Robert said.

"Looks like we'll be learning some new words in America," Jennet said. "Did you know this is a wharf and not a quay?"

"And we will be buying farms, not crofts," James added.

Being the oldest of the three brothers, John always took charge. He was tapping his foot, and Mary could tell he was getting anxious.

"I'd like to just stand here and discuss the English language with you, but there comes another ship," John said. "We dinnae want those passengers to get ahead of us. James, find us lodging at least for tonight, longer if you can. Robert, find us something to eat. I will find the land office and sort out what's required so we can start looking for crofts for sale."

"Don't forget – they're called farms in America," James reminded him.

"Farms, then," John said as he stormed off.

"What's wrong with him?" Robert asked.

"He does not like being corrected by his younger brothers," Mary said. "You should know that better than any of us."

"Let's get to our tasks, wee brother," James said, putting his arm around Robert's shoulder to move him along.

"It's terribly hot here in the sun," Mary said. "Could you not help us by moving these trunks into the shade of that tree over there first?"

Without a word, the men picked up the trunks and put them down on a bricked area under an oak tree. There was lots of foot traffic and goods being pushed by in carts as their ship and the new arrival were unloaded.

Each cart left a different smell in its wake. The ship that just arrived hauled cattle, horses, pigs, and sheep. Mary and Jennet took mental note of the numbers and quality of the livestock. Their husbands would be looking for horses and a wagon.

One cart caught the women's attention as it brought a welcome fragrance of spices. "Cinnamon!" Mary exclaimed.

"Ah, and nutmeg," Jennet said with a sigh.

A breeze picked up coming off the wharf. There was the familiar smell of fish in the air. More comfortable now, Mary and Jennet were lost in private thoughts. A tear ran down Jennet's cheek. She quickly wiped it away, but not before Mary noticed.

"What's the matter?" Mary asked.

"I was just thinking about home and how we'll never see it again."

"Oh aye, the wee toon." Mary said. No more words were needed.

In a few minutes, John and James returned, looking at ease. "Good news," James said. "I found us lodging above a pub just up the way and a job to boot."

"What sort of job?" Jennet asked.

"You're looking at the new stock man for the Knife and Fork Pub... I mean Tavern. They call pubs taverns here."

"And we thought they spoke English!" Mary said. "It seems we shall be learning lots of new words. Congratulations on your new job, James."

James smiled. "I just happened to walk in as the old stock man was quitting all in a huff. I seized the opportunity."

"Pay's reasonable, too," John said. "James told me, so I would know what the going rate is for labor here in the city until we get some land."

"What did you learn at the land office?" Mary asked.

"I got us on the ledger for when they open after lunch. Two-o'clock. There were maps on the walls. The Carolinas, Virginia, western Pennsylvania. Have you seen Robert?"

"No," Mary said.

"No doubt he's found a bonnie lass to talk to," James said. "We could starve for all he cares if that's the case."

"There he comes," Jennet said. "Now, dinnae tease him, James."

Robert's smile stretched from one ear to the other. He walked up to the family and set down a loaf of warm sourdough bread and a wee crock of honey. "There you are," Robert said. He was visibly pleased with himself.

"I dinnae see nary a piece of meat." John cut his eyes and stared at Robert.

"It was a bakery," Robert said. "A bakery sells no meat."

"So why did you go to a bakery for our lunch?" John asked.

"There was a bonnie lass standing –"

"I told you," James said, directing his comments to Jennet. "I told you he had found a bonnie wee lass." They all laughed.

"She's bonnie, but she's not so wee," Robert said. "She's about my age and has the prettiest blue eyes you ever did see. Her name is Sarah. Her father owns the bakery and is the baker. Sarah helps with the baking and the selling."

"Ah!" John said. "One that's bonnie and can cook?"

"Leave him alone, John," Mary said. "Robert, she sounds lovely."

Not realizing how hungry they all were, they managed to eat the entire loaf of bread and every drop of the honey while Robert was still talking about his new love.

"Let's go look at the lodging James found for us and get Mary and Jennet settled in," John said. "We lads have an appointment at two o'clock at the land office."

The five of them divided up the trunks and cloth sacks holding their belongings to walk to the tavern James had found for them for at least a few days. James introduced them to the innkeeper, who told James to show his family upstairs to their room.

The room contained three small beds and one lone straight-back chair. An empty candlestick sat on the wee table. Precious little natural light attempted to enter the room through the grimy four-pane north-facing window.

Mary pinched her nose. "It smells like last night's stinking lodgers are still here."

Being closest to the window, Robert pried it open but it would not budge more than a wee bit. A welcomed breeze soon found its way into the room.

"We will need a candle before the sun sets," Mary said.

"There's a candle shop next to the bakery," Robert said. "I'll purchase what we need."

"I'm sure you will," James said, "since it will give you an excuse to see Sarah." It seemed to Mary that James and John never tired of teasing their young brother.

"It's time for our appointment at the land office," John said. "I'm eager to see what's available in the Carolinas."

With that, the men left. Mary and Jennet pulled back the top coverlets and examined the sheets underneath on the three beds. "They look clean, so they do," Mary said.

Jennet nodded, and they sat down on two of the beds. They faced each other, exhausted beyond words and resigned to more days and weeks of an unknown future.

After a few minutes, Jennet stood up and stretched her back. She started putting some order in the contents of the trunk she and James brought with them.

"If you are trying to shame me into getting off this bed and doing something, it's not working," Mary said. She was too tired to hold her eyes open.

****

"Sit down and tell us what you learned," Mary said as soon as the men returned from the land office several hours later.

The men exchanged glances, their faces not hiding their disappointment.

"You're the oldest, John," Robert said. "You tell them."

"It can't be that bad," Jennet said. "Do tell."

"The land in North Carolina is described as if the roads are lined with gold and the burns run clear with more fish than we could catch in a lifetime," John said.

"But?" Mary asked.

"But the prices are high for sons of a Kintyre tenant crofter," John said. He held up his hand toward Robert's face. "Don't tell me again that I should say farmer."

Robert looked at the floor, his mouth clenched shut, no doubt from his humiliation at being called down by his brother in front of the others.

"It turns out," James said, "that the king has divided up the land amongst his cronies – called Lords Proprietors – and they have agents selling the land mostly in parcels too large for us to purchase."

"What if the three of you went in together on a parcel?" Mary asked.

"It's still too much," John said. "Too much money."

"What are we to do?" Jennet asked.

"Think of another way," James said. "We've come too far to give up on our first day."

"First thing in the morning I will get out and about town and see what our options are," John said. "James has a job here at the tavern and Robert will look for a way to make some money. I will keep my eye out for work. We will save every shilling we can come by until we can buy land somewhere."

"God made a way for us to get to America," Mary said. "He will make a way for us to get by here. We have known nothing but hard times in Kintyre, so we will survive."

"I want to do more than survive!" Robert said, a bit too loudly.

"Dinnae expect too much, Robert," Mary said. "You will just be disappointed. We are all in this together. We will find a way."

Jennet was busy getting some food prepared for supper. The bread Robert brought back from the bakery when he went to the candle shop looked like a feast compared to the fare on the ship. John asked God's blessing on the bread, and they passed it around for each one to tear off a chunk.

***

The following afternoon, John came in with a wee bounce in his step. "Better news today," he said, as he sat down on the bed by the door.

Mary and Jennet put down the socks they were mending and sat down on the bed facing him.

"Tell us!" Mary said. "Dinnae keep us waiting!"

"I talked to a man outside the land office," John said. "He was a Scot and appeared to me to be honest enough. He said we might be better off not dealing with the land office. There are people already in North Carolina who are willing to sell some of their land. They will sell a few acres. If I can come up with enough money to buy a small croft, we can all settle on it and eventually buy more."

"James is dead set on buying land of his own," Jennet said.

"We all are," John said. "But we need to take this one step at a time. We need to find a way to get our foot in the door in North Carolina. It is too crowded here in Pennsylvania. I already know I dinnae want to settle here."

"Nor do I," Jennet said.

"The five of us can think this thing through tonight when James and Robert get in," John said. "I'm feeling better about our options than I did last night."

Just then James tapped on the door, tired from his day of working in the stock room. "You are walking like you have been sampling a wee dram or two," John said as James staggered into the room.

James laughed. "Wish I had," he said. "There was no time for such as that. I'm tired, and my legs still think they are on that ship." He walked to the nearest bed with exaggerated wobbling before flopping down on it. The bed shook with his belly laugh.

"Stocking harder than crofting?" John asked.

"No, I would not say that. A wee bit boring. Too much time inside the building. Not enough fresh air," James said.

"Fresh air?" Jennet asked. "Not much of that in this room either, but more than some days on that ship come to think of it."

"I wonder what kind of a day Robert's had," Mary said. "I hope he found a job."

"He thinks his job is to win the hand of that baker's daughter," John said. "Being sweet on a lass will not put food on the table."

"It put this bread on our table yesterday," Mary said. "Dinnae sell your wee brother short!"

"Feels good to laugh," Jennet said. "There was little to laugh about on the ship between the boredom, the noise, and the seasickness."

"Ah, the seasickness," Mary said. Her body shuddered at the very memory of it.

"What's funny?" Robert asked as he came in.

"Mary was just remembering how much she enjoyed being on that ship," Jennet said. "I think she's homesick for it."

"It's still in the harbor. If you hurry, you might be able to get back on it," Robert said.

Mary shivered but gave him a smile.

***

John and Robert got jobs at the wharf. Mary was none too happy with that. She believed the stories she had heard about the unsavory men who worked such jobs.

"I can keep him in line," Robert said.

"John's not the one I'm worried about," Mary said.

Mary and Jennet were both excellent seamstresses. They sometimes went out together during the day and, after casually passing the bakery on the off chance they would catch a glimpse of Robert and Sarah, carefully spread the word among the local women and shopkeepers that they would welcome piecework.

Mary's specialty was making lace. She soon had regular orders for adding lace to garments and repairing lace.

Jennet was handy with a needle and thread. She was in great demand as word spread about her beautiful work. She could repair ripped dresses in no time at all and the owners were hard pressed to locate the site of the tears after Jennet finished her work.

One night, John burst into the family's room at the tavern. "I have found the perfect piece of land!"

All the family gathered around him. "William Montgomery sought me out this afternoon. He had learned that John and Elisabeth Caldwell –"

"John Caldwell from Southend?" James asked.

"Aye, that John Caldwell! Mr. Caldwell and his wife have land on Caldwell Creek in Mecklenburg County in the piedmont section of the province of North Carolina that they are willing to sell. They would like to sell it to a family they knew back in Southend or Campbeltown."

"How much land?" Robert asked.

"How much money?" Mary asked.

"It is 134 acres on the head waters of Caldwell Creek. It is twenty pounds. Mary and I have that much money. I propose that I purchase the land since I'm the eldest And I propose that the rest of you go in together and purchase a wagon and team of oxen for the journey. Agreed?"

All spoke up in the affirmative.

"Mr. Montgomery said I should send a letter to Mr. Caldwell and tell him we are coming and we want the land. He's not telling anyone else about the land before I talk to him tomorrow to confirm."

They all started talking at once. Mary hugged and kissed John. Jennet was so happy she cried. James and Robert clapped John on the back at first but then gave him bear hugs. Mary scarcely had time to step out of their way.

"Shows how important old friends can be," Robert said.

"Aye," John said. "Who would have dreamt friends of Mother's in Southend would reach out and we would hear about it?"

"When must we leave Pennsylvania?" Robert asked.

"As soon as we get a wagon, a team of oxen, and necessary supplies," John said.

"Mary and I have a good idea what we need," Jennet said. "Perhaps we can buy some things tomorrow." Mary nodded in agreement.

"If the family meeting is over, I need to go somewhere," Robert said.

"You're excused," John said. He winked at Robert. "I hope she says 'yes!'"

"Me, too!" Robert turned to go. "It's her father I'm worried about."

***

Sarah said she'd be honored to marry Robert, and her father gave his blessing. Robert and Sarah called on the Presbyterian minister the next day. He said he would marry them Saturday morning.

While Robert saw to marriage arrangements, James got time away from his work at the tavern to buy a wagon and a team of four oxen.

Mary and Jennet purchased an iron skillet and iron lidded pot from the blacksmith, small barrels of flour and cornmeal from the miller, and fat trimmings from the butcher.

The days passed quickly. By Friday afternoon all supplies had been gathered, employers had been given notice, and acquaintances had been told farewell.

Early Saturday morning the wagon was packed, and the family made their way to the minister's home. The wedding ceremony included a long sermon which had them all fidgeting. Their eagerness to be on their way was lost on the minister.

The sun was high in the sky when the three couples said goodbye to Sarah's father and teary mother. Sarah waved and shed a few tears of her own until the wagon carried them out of her parents' sight. When she could no longer see the buildings of the town, she turned to embrace her husband.

The three couples were quiet – each person lost in their own thoughts about their new adventure, no doubt wondering what pleasures and challenges lay ahead of them on The Great Wagon Road through Maryland, Virginia, and North Carolina.

Author's Note:

I don't know the name of the ship on which John, Mary, James, Jennet, and Robert Morrison sailed from Campbeltown, Scotland to America. I chose the name *The Crimson Arrow* to pay homage to the first ship built at the Campbeltown Shipyard.

The three brothers – John, James, and Robert – were born to William and Janet Hall Morrison in Campbeltown, Scotland. Janet Hall's family lived on Eden Farm on the Mull of Kintyre. Morrisons were tenants on farms in Campbeltown called Crossibeg and Baraskomill when the Hearth Tax records were made in the 1690s and early 1700s. (It was called a Hearth Tax because you were taxed if there was smoke coming out of the chimney of your house!) The Duke of Argyll owned Kintyre, so everyone living there were his tenants.

I know nothing of this Morrison family's life or length of time in Pennsylvania or how they went about buying land in Mecklenburg County, NC in the 1760s. Their names, the names of the crofts on which Halls and Morrisons were tenants in the 1690s and early 1700s on the Kintyre Peninsula of Scotland, the names of places in Scotland, the names of John and Elisabeth Caldwell from whom John Morrison purchased his first 134 acres of land on the headwaters of Caldwell Creek, and the fact that they would have passed Fair Head as they sailed through the North Channel are all true. Since the Caldwells came from Southend, the Morrisons would have known them. I do not know the details of how John Morrison made arrangements to buy his first land from John and Elisabeth Caldwell. Aside from those things, this is a work of fiction.

Robert Morrison, the youngest brother, married a young woman named Sarah. It is not known where they met. Their first child, a son, was born in Pennsylvania in 1763, according to his American Revolutionary War pension affidavit. To have Robert and Sarah meet, get married, and have a child would have necessitated a much longer and more involved short story, so I took literary license and did not include the birth of their first child.

Each of the three brothers purchased land and established farms in Mecklenburg County, North Carolina. Robert served in the Revolutionary War. John and James were patriots, too.

According to his 1777 estate papers, John owned an inordinate amount of lead and gunpowder. It is speculated that he was stockpiling munitions for the war and was ambushed by Tories and mortally wounded the last week in August 1777.

John and Mary Morrison were my great-great-great-great-grandparents. I wrote this short story to honor them and how they set my family on a wonderful path in America. I have been privileged to live most of my life on a bit of the land John Morrison purchased in North Carolina in the 1760s and 1770s.

I was privileged in the early 1990s to visit Campbeltown and Southend, to walk on the Crossibeg and Eden crofts, and to take a day trip on the passenger ferry which ran between Campbeltown, Scotland and Ballycastle, Northern Ireland. To look back on "the wee toon" of Campbeltown from the ferry much as my Morrison ancestors would have looked upon it for the last time in the early 1760s was an emotional event for me. As I looked up at Fair Head towering above the North Channel, I could only imagine what an awe-inspiring sight it would have been for them.

A piece of my heart remains there, as it undoubtedly forever did for my ancestors and their friends and acquaintances from Kintyre who also settled the Rocky River section of present-day Cabarrus and Mecklenburg counties in North Carolina.

WHOM CAN WE TRUST?

Mecklenburg County, North Carolina
May 1775

Archibald McCurdy came into the log cabin on Saturday afternoon and flopped down in his rocking chair by the stone hearth without speaking to his wife, Maggie.

"You look like you have bad news," Maggie said. At 20 years old, she was four years her husband's junior. She wiped her floured hands on her apron and with the backs of her hands she pushed back the strands of hair that had escaped her cap before sitting down beside Archie.

"Not necessarily bad news," he said. "Just news that's a wee bit concerning."

Maggie rested her hand on Archie's forearm. She searched his eyes. "What is it?"

"Colonel Polk has called for that county meeting we've been expecting. He's calling it a convention. Every militia company has to elect two men to attend as delegates. It's scheduled for Friday, May 19 at the courthouse."

"Things aren't getting any better with Governor Martin?"

"No, things are getting worse with him. And the king. The militia will meet after worship on Sunday. I started helping to spread the word on my way home this afternoon."

"What do you think will come out of this?"

"Rev. Balch has been meeting with Dr. Brevard and others at Queen's Museum this spring and maybe a couple of times at Alexandriana. A lawyer from Salisbury, William Kennon, has met with them."

"You've known this?" Maggie asked. "Why didn't you tell me?"

Archie shrugged. "I was hoping nothing would come of it, and they were meeting secretly so as not to draw attention. The fewer people that knew, the better."

"What have they been doing?" Maggie asked.

"It's said they've been drawing up a document to be voted on at the county convention. A document to state our grievances against the Crown."

"The governor won't take kindly to that!" Maggie laughed.

"No doubt about that. I have a bad feeling about this. We'll likely all be labeled enemies of the king after this convention – not just the lads who blew up the king's gunpowder four years ago."

Archie leaned back in his chair, closed his eyes, and exhaled audibly. Maggie patted his arm and returned to her bread dough.

She picked up the dough and slapped it down on the table. She kneaded the dough with authority and muttered under her breath.

Archie spun around in his chair. "I didn't mean to upset you, Maggie."

"What did you expect?"

"You hum sometimes as you knead dough, but all I hear now is a lot of noise."

"Sometimes I take the opportunity to get all my worries out. I'm imaging the governor's face on this dough and I'm taking great delight in punching it and slamming it on the table. You let out your concerns by going outside and walking around the farm. I take care of mine by making bread."

***

Maggie woke up before the sun on Sunday morning. She sighed and turned to find Archie's side of the bed empty, the warmth of his body long gone.

Her eyes gradually adjusted to the pre-dawn light of the waning moon coming through the window. She reached for her shawl and followed the soft orange glow of the embers in the fireplace in the other room of the log cabin. She could just make out the outline of her husband sitting in his rocking chair, his head bowed. She thought he was sleeping, but then she realized his lips were moving. He was praying. She held back at the door and watched him and hugged herself against the morning chill.

The hot coals crackled. Archie stirred and stretched. Maggie stepped forward and softly cleared her throat. Archie turned toward her.

"You're up mighty early," Maggie said. "Long night?"

"Aye. Couldn't sleep," Archie said. "You?"

Maggie sat on the chair beside his and squeezed his forearm. "I slept until just now." She yawned. "Did you sleep at all?"

"Just a wee bit early on. Then I woke up and couldn't go back to sleep, so I came out here. Do you know how irritating it is to lie there wide awake next to someone sleeping away?" He laughed.

"Aye, I know that feeling very well." Maggie laughed with him.

Archie started rocking his chair. Maggie snuggled up to his side and rested her head on his shoulder. "What's going to happen," she asked.

"Everything points toward war with Britain."

"But we have no army to fight the strongest country in the world! They will squash us like a bug!"

"Do you know what you said?" Archie asked. He stopped the rocking chair.

"Aye, I know what –"

"No, Maggie." Archie folded his hands around hers. "You said, 'They will squash us.'" Then more slowly, emphasizing the first word, "They will squash us. We're still part of Britain, but you called the British, 'They.' See, Maggie? If people like you – like us – already feel the split between the colonies and Britain, how else can the divide be settled any way short of war?"

Maggie's eyes stung with tears. She willed them not to escape her eyelids. She and Archie stared at each other for several minutes, each one nodding in recognition of the gravity of the situation.

A rooster crowed. "Time to start our day," Maggie said. She stood and leaned over to kiss Archie on the cheek, then reached for a cloth looped over a metal hook beside the stone chimney. She lifted the heavy iron lid off the pot of porridge hanging from the crane in the fireplace and set it on the hearth. She peered into the pot and announced that breakfast was ready.

Maggie dipped the steaming hot porridge into two wooden bowls she had taken from the cupboard the night before and set on the table with two pewter spoons. She uncovered the bowl of wild strawberries picked the day before and invited her husband to help himself to this wonderful springtime treat.

"I thought I smelled strawberries," he said.

"I picked them while you were gone yesterday. Thought I'd save them for this morning."

"There's nothing better after a long hard winter."

Maggie spooned berries on top of her porridge and reached across the table. They held hands and Archie thanked God for the porridge and berries and asked Him to guide him and the other militia members in their meeting after worship later that day.

They ate in silence. Maggie was lost in her thoughts and Archie appeared to be the same. When they finished eating, Maggie cleared the dirty dishes from the table and set about to pack a picnic lunch for them to take to church.

"I'll go milk the cow and take the milk to the springhouse," Archie said.

"Don't forget to gather eggs. I hope there are at least four."

***

Maggie hurried to the bedroom to get dressed while Archie was out doing chores. She put on a shift and then inhaled to make it easier to get into her stays. She tied her stockings on above her knees and tied her shoes. Her two linsey-woolsey petticoats were put on after the stays so the stays would hold the weight of the petticoats. There was still a chill in the air, so she put on a quilted bodice for added warmth under her best blue silk gown.

The gown was her favorite and never failed to prompt Archie to comment about how it matched her eyes. She folded her square handkerchief into a triangle. After centering the point of the triangle best she could in the center of the top of her gown, she tucked the ends of the handkerchief into her bodice and checked the look in her looking glass. After all, she was going to church and had to take extra pains for modesty's sake.

Maggie brushed her hair and piled it on top of her head. Just as she was securing her Sunday hat with a hairpin, she heard Archie come in the front door.

"Don't you look bonnie!" Archie said when Maggie entered the sitting room. "That gown exactly matches your beautiful blue eyes." Archie's arms encircled her waist and he knocked her hat cattywampus when he kissed her passionately on the mouth.

"Archie!" she said, attempting to catch her breath.

"Too bad we have to go to church," he said. "Seems much more pleasant to stay here." He kissed her again while she straightened her hat.

"You have a meeting after worship, remember?" she asked. "Go get dressed."

"You aren't very obliging this morning."

"Can't help it. Get dressed or we'll be late."

While Archie put on his best clothes, Maggie picked up the basket containing their lunch items and went out onto the front porch. Their mixed dog, Laddie, met her at the door wagging his tail with great enthusiasm. She adored the dog and it was obvious he loved her at least as much.

The two horses hitched to Archie's most beautiful wagon whinnied at the sight and sound of Maggie talking to Laddie. Maggie chuckled when she saw the hand-painted sign Archie had hung on the back of the wagon; "A. McCurdy. Blacksmith and Wagonmaker."

In an effort to distract Laddie from the basket of ham biscuits and strawberries, she scratched behind his ears. He was almost relaxed into a nap when Archie came outside.

"I see you are taking your new sign today. Don't you think everyone at Rocky River Meeting House knows what you do?"

"You never know when a new settler in need of a wagon or blacksmith work is going to be there. If I do not have a sign on the wagon, how will they know I am a blacksmith and wagon maker?"

"I suppose that's true," Maggie said as Archie helped her up onto the wagon seat.

It was a beautiful spring morning. Maggie slipped her arm under Archie's elbow. Cardinals and robins provided their distinctive music as they traveled along the red dirt road. A woodpecker worked on a tree trunk in the distance. The poplar trees were in full bloom and the road was dotted with the blossoms that had dropped off. The blooms looked like green tulips with yellow centers outlined in orange.

As they approached the log meeting house set on a hill above the Rocky River, Archie turned to Maggie and said, "Be careful who you talk to and what you say. I'm not certain yet who truly sees things the way we see them."

"I'll be careful not to speak my mind," Maggie said.

Archie rolled his eyes at her. "You always speak your mind."

"That's what you love about me," she said, matter-of-factly. Archie winked at her.

***

After the worship service, Rev. Balch greeted each of the congregants as they exited the door. As the women and children gathered in small groups for conversation in the shade of the oak, ash, maple, and hickory trees, the able-bodied men returned to the sanctuary for their militia meeting.

Maggie kept Archie's admonitions in mind and made small talk with her friends. One mentioned picking the first strawberries of the season the afternoon before. She and Maggie compared their expectations for the year's crop and how good a cobbler would taste.

"The house smelled like strawberries when I woke up this morning," Maggie said. "Archie was up early and thought he smelled them. I'm surprised there were any left for our porridge. He can't resist a strawberry."

Another friend commented how tired she was of making bread. "I tried sprinkling the top of yesterday's loaf with brown sugar, just to have something a little different."

"How did it turn out?" Maggie asked.

"The sugar burned!" the woman said. "It smelled terrible and we couldn't eat the top crust. I had to go outside and scrape the sugar off. The chickens loved it!" The small circle of women all laughed.

"I'm sure that has happened to all of us," one of the women said. "It's certainly happened to me."

"How can we speak of such mundane things while the men are meeting about the tensions between the colonies and the king?" another woman blurted out. The circle of women stood silent for a few seconds. Maggie tried to read the faces of the others without showing her own feelings.

"I agree," Maggie said. "This affects us just as much as it does the men."

The church door squeaked open and Maggie turned to watch for Archie. He and the other younger men in their early twenties were among the first to come out into the church grove.

Without further comment on the subject of the militia meeting, the women said their goodbyes, and Maggie made her way through the crowd to meet Archie on the path to where they'd left their wagon. Maggie retrieved her picnic basket from the back of the wagon and Archie picked up the jug of cool spring water they'd brought from home.

They usually ate their dinner on the way home from church. Maggie leaned down and started to open the basket but stopped. She sat up straight and turned toward Archie as he instructed the horses to pull the wagon toward the road. "What can you tell me?" she asked.

"Not much. I'm not allowed to say who our delegates are."

"Are you one of them?"

"No."

They rode in silence for several miles, the only sounds being the clop-chop of the horses' hooves on the rutted red dirt road, the occasional squeak of a wagon wheel, and the cheerful sound of cardinals, chickadees, and mockingbirds in the woods they passed.

"Hungry?" Maggie asked.

"I could eat," Archie said.

Maggie leaned down and reached into the picnic basket for the ham biscuits she had made the night before. Maggie knew not to ask any more questions. If Archie wanted her to know anything about the meeting or the upcoming convention, he would tell her. If she needed to know, she knew he would tell her.

***

A rooster crowed at sunrise on Friday, May 19. Maggie turned in bed and found Archie's pillow vacant again. She stretched and sat up in bed. It promised to be a long day. She bowed her head and prayed there would not be a war as a result of today's convention in Charlottetown.

She dressed and went to the other room where Archie sat in his rocking chair. "Morning," she said softly so she wouldn't startle him.

Archie turned toward her. "Morning."

Maggie walked up behind him and rubbed his shoulders. "Did you sleep at all?"

"Some."

She leaned down and kissed his cheek.

"I should have gone," he said. "I should have gone!" He clenched his teeth and fists and pounded on the arms of his chair. "I can't just sit here or piddle around on the farm all day while that convention is going on fifteen miles away and I don't know what's happening!" He jumped up, knocking the back of the rocker into Maggie. She took a step back and grabbed the top of the chair to keep from falling backwards. Archie beat on the stone chimney.

"I thought only the delegates were going," Maggie said.

"They're the only ones allowed in the courthouse, but anyone can go and stand outside and listen. I should be there."

"What about plowing my garden spot? You promised to do it today if it was dry enough."

Archie said nothing, so Maggie went to the corner cupboard and took out two bowls and spoons and placed them on the table. She picked up a cloth from a hook beside the chimney and stepped toward the fireplace. Archie stood in the way of her getting to the pot of porridge. She stood there for a minute or more, wishing he'd realize he needed to move away from the hearth.

"Archie!" Maggie said with more emphasis on "chie" than she would in a normal tone. "Please move so I can get the porridge!"

Archie stepped aside. "Why are you so angry?"

"I'm not angry! It's frustrating when you know I'm trying to get to the fireplace to a put a meal on the table and you just stand there in the way."

"I can't read your mind!"

"Why else would I be standing here with a cloth in my hand at day-break?"

"I don't know," Archie said.

Maggie let out an audible sigh and shook her head. She mumbled under her breath. *I don't know. I can't read your mind!* She swung the crane toward herself and lifted the hot iron pot from it. She set it on the table, removed the lid, and stirred the porridge.

She and Archie sat down at the table. As Maggie spooned the steaming porridge into their bowls, she took a deep breath and let it out slowly. "I'm sorry," she said. "I'm sorry I lost my temper. I didn't realize how nervous I was over the convention."

"Me, too," Archie said. "We're both uneasy. I forget this affects you as much as it does me."

"Maybe more so. At least you have a better idea about what's going on today. Are you going?"

"No, it's too late in the morning to get started. William White said he'd come by on his way home and tell me what happened. I have work to do. I'd better get to it after we eat."

***

Maggie looked out the window that evening. The sun had set behind the woods and she could scarcely make out Archie. He was outside watching for William to come by with news from the convention. He paced back and forth. Laddie paced with him for a while, then lay down, no doubt concerned. It wasn't like Archie to walk back and forth in the yard in the twilight. Maggie wanted to call Archie inside to eat supper, but he had a mind of his own – as did she.

Just then, William rode up on his horse. He dismounted and Archie offered the horse a bucket of water. Maggie watched as the two men talked. William was very animated. *I wish I could hear what he's saying! Archie better tell me everything!*

When William got back on his horse, Maggie hurried away from the window and sat down by the hearth where she kept her sewing basket and clothes that needed mending. By the time Archie came inside, Maggie had finished sewing a button on Archie's vest and was biting the thread off. She tried her best to look like she'd been sewing the whole time he was outside.

"It's coming to a boil," Archie said. "They wrote a document and it's being polished tonight and readied for a vote tomorrow."

"What time will you be rising in the morning?"

"What?"

"I know you're going to the courthouse. I just need to know what time to have your porridge ready."

"You know me well. I need to leave by four o'clock."

Maggie stared into Archie's eyes. Neither of them spoke for several minutes.

"I know you are curious," Archie said.

"Of course."

Archie was silent for several minutes. Maggie could tell he was searching for words. "It states our grievances against the Crown and declares that Mecklenburg County is free and independent."

Maggie swallowed hard and fought the tears that began to sting her eyes.

"Let's eat," she said, "and then we'd better get some sleep."

***

Maggie shot up in bed in the middle of the night. Archie's side of the bed was empty. *Have I slept so long that he's gone?* She jumped out of bed and rushed through the door to find Archie rocking in his chair.

"What time is it?" Maggie asked, rushing to grab bowls and spoons from the corner cupboard.

"It's only two-thirty," Archie said, putting his pocket watch back in his pocket. "I can't sleep, so I might as well go on and leave. I'll milk the cow and saddle up Chestnut while you get the porridge on the table."

Maggie pulled her hair back and quickly braided it to be out of her way. She set a cast iron skillet on the hot coals and added some fat. While the skillet heated, she mixed some flour, cornmeal, egg, and buttermilk into a batter for johnny cakes. When the grease was shimmering hot, she spooned the batter in clumps into the skillet. She moved the pot of porridge from the crane in the fireplace and set it directly on the hot coals to hurry up the cooking.

By the time Archie came back from the barn with a bucket of milk, Maggie had his bowl of porridge on the table along with a few strawberries she had held back from the day before. She was fanning the johnny cakes with her apron.

"Chestnut must not be too happy being roused this early," Maggie said.

"Not too happy with me," Archie said. He sat at his usual place at the table. "Aren't you eating?"

"I'll eat after you're gone. I'm trying to get the johnny cakes cool so they won't sweat and get soggy. I trust you filled your canteen at the spring. What else do I need to get for your travel?

"You've thought of everything," Archie said. "Come. Catch your breath. You're rushing about in all directions."

"I need to get these cakes packed for you," she said, reaching for a cloth bag she had made just for this purpose. "I must be forgetting something."

"Come, Maggie. Sit with me. Let's have a prayer."

Maggie sat across the table from her husband and reached out to take his waiting hands in hers. Archie thanked God for the food Maggie had prepared and God had provided.

While Archie ate, Maggie brought her Psalter to the table and turned to the twenty-third Psalm. As she started to read, Archie put down his spoon and gave her his full attention.

"The Lord's my shepherd, I'll not want. He makes me down to lie in pastures green: he leadeth me the quiet waters by. My soul he doth restore again; and me to walk doth make within the paths of right-eousness, e'en for his own name's sake. Yea, though I walk in death's dark vale, yet will I feel none ill; For thou art with me, and thy rod and staff me comfort still. My table thou hast furnished in presence of my foes; My head with oil thou dost anoint, and my cup overflows. Goodness and mercy all my life shall surely follow me; And in God's house for evermore my dwelling-place shall be."

With the reading of the last sentence, Maggie's voice broke. She hur-riedly wiped a tear from her cheek and swallowed hard to steel herself.

"Let's pray again," Archie said. He and Maggie reached across the table and held one another's hands. "Our dear heavenly Father," Archie prayed, "be with us today as we go about our chores. Be with Maggie in my absence, and go with me as I travel. We pray for the delegates to today's convention. It's a grave matter they will discuss and vote on. Lead them to act within your will, O God. Be in our thinking, in our speaking, and in our doing. We ask in the name of Jesus. Amen."

They held hands for a few minutes longer. "I guess I should get a move on," Archie said. They got up from the table. "Be safe, Maggie." He hugged her tight and held her in his arms. "Take no chances. Stay alert. Take the musket with you if you go to the loom house or strawberry field."

"I will," she whispered as she rested her head on his chest.

Archie held her tight and kissed the top of her head. "If I'm not home by dark, don't fret. The vote might not be taken until late in the evening. You never know how long things like this might last."

"But we've never had a thing like this before," she said.

Archie nodded, and Maggie slipped from his embrace. She hurried to put the johnny cakes in the bag and handed it to him. They walked outside in silence. Archie secured the johnny cakes in a saddle bag while Maggie stroked the horse's cheek. "Take care of him, Chestnut," she whispered.

She watched Archie settle into the saddle. Their eyes met. "Love you," Maggie said.

"Love you, too." Archie nodded and winked.

Maggie watched until Archie's silhouette was swallowed by the darkness.

After eating breakfast, Maggie went to the loom house to continue weaving the linen cloth she was making from the flax she and Archie had grown on their farm. She worked the loom until her shoulders ached. She picked up the musket and walked down the hill to the creek. She lingered there, stretching her tired back. Sunlight dappled through the leaves and danced on the water and the creek bank. She closed her eyes and tried to just relax as the water splashed over rocks and tree roots, but she could think of nothing but what was taking place at the courthouse.

Realizing this wasn't getting the strawberries picked, she returned to the house to retrieve a wooden bucket. Fresh strawberries would be a nice treat for Archie when he got home that night. As she picked the berries, she wondered what lay ahead for her sparsely-settled community.

Later in the day, Maggie prepared supper. She boiled potatoes and cabbage in the fireplace. Colcannon was one of her favorite dishes to make and Archie liked it, too. She picked a variety of greens in her kitchen garden. The last of the ham would taste good with the colcannon. Archie would be hungry from his day at the courthouse and long ride home. She had been too nervous to eat anything all day, but she thought she would have an appetite after Archie got home safe and sound. It was getting dark when she heard his familiar whistle.

Maggie grabbed a lantern, lit it, and hurried to catch up with Archie at the barn. She saw his bowed head and slumped shoulders as he removed his saddle from his horse. She knew from his demeanor that he did not have good news.

"Archie?" Maggie said.

He turned to look at her and slowly turned his head from side to side. No words were necessary.

As soon as Archie settled his horse for the night, Maggie walked up to him and put her arms around him. They held each other and Archie rested his chin on the top of Maggie's head. After a few minutes, Maggie lifted her head and looked up into Archie's furrowed face. "Let's go," she said. "Supper's ready."

Maggie could feel Archie's eyes on her as she stirred the potatoes and cabbage together and poured hot melted fat over the bowl of greens to make a wilted salad. She brought the hot dishes to the table and they sat down. After Archie thanked God for the food and the safety He had granted both of them, he told Maggie some of what had happened that day. Maggie still had little appetite, but she was happy to see Archie eating well. She was more interested in what Archie had to say than the food on her plate.

"It's done," Archie said. "I stood there at the foot of the courthouse steps and heard a declaration of independence read. Mecklenburg County declared its independence from Great Britain today. There's going to be war. People will take sides. We need to make a mental list of whom we can trust."

Author's Note:

McCurdy family tradition indicates that Archibald and Maggie Sellers McCurdy built their log house in 1773. It stood for more than 200 years in the Flowes Store section of present-day Cabarrus County until vandals burned it down. (Cabarrus was formed in 1792 out of Mecklenburg County.) The house was on the National Register of Historic Places.

The original house had one room with an attic. Mud filled the gaps between the logs. Half-dovetail notches joined the corners. A second room was added. A new fireplace was opened in the chimney to give that room access to the warmth of a fire. That arrangement was known as a "saddlebag" plan. The house had front doors and back doors. The original dwelling had but two small windows.

Out buildings on the McCurdy's farm included a loom house, a smokehouse, a corn crib, and a log barn.

It is said that Archibald McCurdy stood on the steps of the Mecklenburg County Courthouse on May 20, 1775, and heard the Mecklenburg Declaration of Independence read. When he got home, he and Maggie listed everyone they knew who could be trusted in the coming fight for American independence.

In 1775, Archibald was among the first to enlist in the Foot Militia of The American Revolution. He fought in the battles of Cowpens, Hanging Rock, Camden, and Rugley's Mill.

Maggie was a true patriot in her own right. The British and Tories called her the "she-rebel" or "she-devil." Many attempts were made on her life. A band of Tories came to her house once, set on killing her. She lifted a board in the floor, allowing her two children, Samuel and Mary, and herself to crawl under the house. They hid there until the Tories left.

On another occasion, Maggie overheard a British and Tory plot to attack the American soldiers encamped about ten miles from her home. The attack was set for midnight and it was now late afternoon. By the time she reached her home it was almost dark and no time could be lost. She quickly donned Archie's clothing, ran to the barn, saddled a horse, and rode off into the night. She was challenged as she rode through the edge of a British camp, but she was allowed to pass because she had also overheard the password. It had been raining heavily and the creeks were swollen. She coaxed her horse through the rushing waters. Just before midnight, she reached the American encampment. Wet and disheveled and wearing Archie's clothing, she had trouble convincing General Nathanael Greene of her identity. The General summoned the officer in command. Imagine Maggie's relief when that officer turned out to be Lieutenant Archibald McCurdy. As a direct result of her warning, the Americans succeeded in defeating the British attack that night, even though they were greatly outnumbered.

Captain Archibald McCurdy was an elder at Rocky River Presbyterian Church. He was elected to the North Carolina General Assembly in 1802 and was a "wagonshire" and blacksmith by trade.

Archibald McCurdy is buried in Spears Graveyard in Cabarrus County, North Carolina.

GO FIGHT, JOHNNY!

Kings Mountain, South Carolina
December 1823

"Wipe your shoes, Jane!" Grace called out as her five-year-old daughter ran up the steps of John Calvin McElwee's two-story log house. Jane stretched to reach up to open the door. "I'm here!" she shouted as she pushed the heavy oak door open. She ran into the sitting room and into the arms of her grandfather.

Jane's parents, Grace and Jim followed, apologizing for Jane's lack of manners. Jim took off his hat, and Grace removed her scarf and shook the snow off. They took off their coats and hung them on hooks by the door. "When you visit someone, you're supposed to knock on the door and wait for them to open it to let you come inside," Grace said.

"You didn't knock on the door before you came in," Jane said, stamping her foot on the wide pine floor boards.

Grace and Jim looked each other. "That's true, honey, but you'd already opened the door and come inside," Grace said. "Come here. Let me help you with your coat and scarf."

Jane obeyed and quickly wiggled out of her coat. She shivered.

"I half expected Clark's Fork to be frozen over," Jim said.

"Pretty early in the season for that," John said.

"Sure feels cold enough," Grace said.

"Grandpa, I have a question and then will you tell me a story?" Jane asked.

"Of course I will. Let's sit in my rocking chair. I'll share my blanket with you."

Jane waited for her grandpa to get settled in his chair. When he held out his arms to her, she crawled onto his lap. He kissed the top of her head and complimented her pigtails.

"What's your question?" John asked.

"I was thinking about something. Our house only has one front door, but your house has two. Why?"

"There's a very good reason for that," John said. "I'm a weaver. You've seen my loom in the other room, haven't you?"

"I didn't know what it was. What's a loom?"

"It's an apparatus that takes yarn or thread or most any kind of pliable fiber and weaves the fibers together to make cloth. Then women like your mother and grandmother take cloth and make clothes."

Jane was quiet for several minutes. The only sound in the house was the popping and crackling of the fire in the fireplace. Jane stared at the fire, but her mind was digesting her grandfather's description of a loom. "What's an appa--?"

"Apparatus?" John asked

"Yes."

"It's a thing you can use to do things with." All three adults in the room laughed.

"She never runs out of questions," Grace said. "It's either why, what, when, or where, and sometimes you just run out of answers."

"Like I just did on apparatus," John said.

"Are you laughing at me, Grandpa?" Jane asked.

"No, honey. I'm laughing at myself. I work on that loom six days-a-week, but you sure tripped me up when you asked me what it is. Would you like for me to show you how it works?"

"Maybe later," Jane said. "You still haven't answered my first question."

"I'm sorry, but I don't even remember what the question was," John said.

"Why does your house have two front doors?"

John laughed. "Oh yes. That's what got me talking about my loom. Like I said, I'm a weaver. I sit at that loom and make cloth. People come to buy cloth from me and I did not want them traipsing through this room with their boots caked in mud and sand to do business with me. Your Grandma wouldn't cotton to that, so I built a house with two front doors."

"Oh." Jane studied her grandfather's eyebrows and hair.

"Why is your hair white?"

"Because I'm old."

"How old are you?"

"Jane!" Grace exclaimed. She squeezed her eyes shut and rubbed her forehead, partially covering her eyes. "It is not polite to ask a person how old they are."

Jane felt tears come to her eyes. "I'm sorry. I didn't know." She turned her face away from her parents and John. "I didn't mean to hurt your feelings, Grandpa."

"Since you are my granddaughter, I don't mind telling you. I'm in my 59th year."

Jane tried to think how many that was. "I'm five. I don't understand fifty-nine."

"I don't understand it either sometimes," John said. Grace and Jim laughed with him. "Since I can't interest you in watching me weave, what story did you want to hear?"

"The one about that time you almost turned around, but your mother told you to go fight!" Jane punched the air with her fist.

"Jane, you shouldn't make Grandpa tell that story every time you see him," Jim said. "Mr. McElwee, you don't have to repeat it if you don't want to. Jane, your grandpa probably has lots of stories he could tell you."

"I don't mind," John said. "After all, I know she expects it and enjoys it."

"It was an exciting day – the day the American Revolution came right here to Kings Mountain."

Jane reached up and rubbed up the prickly whiskers on his unshaven cheek. It made her laugh. John's blue eyes crinkled almost shut as he laughed with her.

"What's all the commotion in here?" John's wife, Margaret asked, appearing at the door from the back bedroom with a big smile.

"Grandma!" Jane squealed, and she jumped off John's lap and ran to hug Margaret. Margaret's arms enveloped the child, then she released her and stepped back.

"I think you've grown since I saw you at church last Sunday!" Margaret said.

"You really think so?" Jane asked.

"It's the truth." Margaret studied Jane's face, then looked her up and down. "You have grown! You were just a wee rabbit on Sunday."

Jane giggled. "Grandma, you're just saying that."

"Maybe I stretched the truth just a wee bit. How about you come with me to the kitchen house and help me make cookies?"

Grandpa's war story forgotten, Jane took Margaret's hand and off they went.

"Don't forget your coat and scarf!" Grace called after them. "You'll freeze between the house and the kitchen!"

Jane skipped back into the parlor, grabbed her blue wool coat and the matching scarf her mother had knitted, and skipped back out of the room. "Wait for me, Grandma!"

***

"Well, I guess it's just the three of us," Grace said. She and Jim sat in homemade ladder-back chairs facing the fireplace. With their chatterbox daughter gone with her grandma, they settled in for a visit with Grace's father.

"Looks like it," John said. "My stories can wait. Margaret will love having Jane's help. She adores that little girl."

"I can tell," Grace said. "And I love Margaret, too. She's the only mother I really remember."

"You must have known some hard times, Mr. McElwee," Jim said.

"It was tough until Margaret agreed to take us all on," John said. "She was mighty brave. She was barely grown herself."

"She was a wonderful mother to me," Grace said. "I couldn't have asked for a better one."

"I've been blessed with two good wives," John said. "The Lord's been good to me. Even in the Battle of Kings Mountain, the Lord took care of Papa, William, and me.

"Speaking of your tough times, Mr. McElwee," Jim said, "Please don't mention that tulip tree on which ten Tories were hanged the day after the battle."

"That's right, Papa," Grace said. "Jane overheard you talking about it during our last visit and she had nightmares for a week."

"I'm sorry I upset her," John said. "You know I did not have any idea she was hearing me."

"We know that, Mr. McElwee," Jim said. "Just wanted to mention it so you'll be careful not to talk about it today."

"Or anytime again until Jane is old enough to handle it," Grace said. "She doesn't have a bucket to carry gory stories in yet."

"I'll be careful," John said. "When she's older, though, she needs to know about the hangings. I think those hangings did more to break the spirit of Loyalists in the area than losing the battle. The war finally took a turn here."

"Are you ready to talk about the battle itself, Papa?" Grace asked. "I don't want to push you, but you've never told us what happened after you turned back around and followed Grandpa and Uncle William to the mountain."

John took a deep breath and slowly exhaled. He leaned his head back and slowly looked around the room, although he did not appear to be focusing on or looking for anything. "You know, it was one of the few battles in the war that was fought almost entirely by Americans. Americans fighting Americans. Maybe the British should have stayed home and just let Americans settle it amongst ourselves."

"I'd never thought about it like that," Grace said. "You might be right, Papa."

"That day was exciting and frightening all at the same time. I was just in my sixteenth year. I'd never seen anything like it, of course. None of us had. Musket balls coming in our direction and bullets from hunting rifles flying in the other direction, pinging off boulders and skinning the bark off trees. Our hunting rifles were more accurate than the muskets those other fellows were using, but I did not know whether to run, hide, or shoot. Then, I thought about Mama back here at the house and James laid up and not able to fight or hardly walk. I knew I had to do my part."

All was quiet for several minutes except for the crackling of the fire. John seemed to stare ahead, yet not be seeing anything but his memories. Once in a while he blinked or flicked a tear from his cheek.

"I've never asked you, Mr. McElwee, did you see Major Ferguson that day?" Jim asked.

"Oh, aye. Word spread through the ranks to be on the lookout for him. They said he would hold his sword in his left hand and he'd be wearing a light hunting shirt. I learned later that he was actually right-handed, but that hand had been shattered at the battle at Brandywine."

"So, you saw him?" Jim asked. "You actually saw the man who invented the flintlock rifle!"

"In the flesh. He was a sight to behold. But let me tell you, those Over Mountain men were a force to be reckoned with. When one of Sevier's men that was wounded – he was way up ahead of me – when he saw Ferguson coming, he yelled for one of his buddies to shoot Ferguson. That fella took aim with his rifle and 'POW!' Ferguson fell off his horse. He wasn't the only one that shot Ferguson, though. He was shot a half-dozen times I reckon."

"I've seen the wooden marker at the northeast end of the mountain that marks the place," Jim said.

"I want to take Jane over there when she's a little older and ready to understand some of the gorier parts of the battle," John said. "I want to show her that boulder that's so shot up – the one they called Ferguson's dining table. Time's coming when all us boys in the battle will be gone and our stories will disappear with us. I want Jane to know what happened."

"We do, too, Papa," Grace said. "She needs to know everything you can tell her. I'm glad you're able to talk about it. There have been so many times I wanted to ask questions about that day, but--"

"But Margaret told you not to," John said.

"Yes." Grace nodded emphatically. "She said the memories were too raw and you would tell me when you were good and ready."

"Your mother and Margaret both tried to protect me from my memories, but a fella cannot forget what he sees and hears in battle."

"I don't understand why Ferguson's men got so confused when he went down," Jim said. "Why didn't they look for orders from his second-in-command?"

"Most of his men were Tories. They weren't trained British troops. He collected volunteers as he went along. He got overconfident at Gilbertstown and gave a bunch of the men furloughs so they could go home for a visit. By the time he learned the Back Water or Over Mountain Men were approaching, it was too late for him to call those men back into service."

"But didn't he have a second-in-command? Didn't he know what to do when Ferguson went down?" Jim asked.

"He immediately raised his white handkerchief in defeat and called for quarter," John said. "The surrender was underway, but some of our men kept shooting. Some claimed they did not know what a white flag or handkerchief meant. I knew what it meant, and I was but fifteen years old!"

Grace turned toward Jim and whispered, "Don't get him riled up."

"In a short while," John continued, "the Tories were ordered into a space about sixty yards long and thirty-five to forty feet wide. Their officers were ordered to stand by rank and the others were ordered to sit on the ground. There weren't any more shots taken. The battle was over. It seemed like the fighting lasted all day, but they say it only lasted an hour. We'd charge up the mountain and run back down. Charge up the mountain and run back down. Charge up the mountain and run back down. We did that three times. Everybody – especially the old men – were too tired to keep going but too afraid to stop. It was quite a day."

John appeared to be lost in his thoughts again, but after a few minutes Grace spoke just above a whisper. "That's the most I've heard you talk about the battle. Thank you."

"The memories of some of the things I saw were too fresh and not for a wee girl's ears," John said. "There are parts I'll never speak of. I was still a bit of a lad myself. I'd seen hogs and chickens slaughtered, but that was the day I saw men slaughtered. Some not much older than me. When I close my eyes to sleep at night, I can still see them. I can still smell the gunpowder. I can still smell the metallic odor of blood. Worst of all, I can still hear their cries of anguish. Some of them calling out their wife's name. Some calling for their mother."

With that, John stared at the fire dying down in the fireplace, lost in his memories. Grace saw a tear slide down his cheek before he leaned back in his chair and closed his eyes. Tears stung her eyes, too, as she watched her father. He grimaced occasionally or shook his head ever so slowly. She could only imagine the sights and sounds inside his head as he, no doubt, relived the day the American Revolution came to Kings Mountain.

Jim got up and added a hickory log to the fire. He poked at the glowing orange coals and blew on them until the flame sputtered back to life. John did not stir. Jim smiled at Grace as he returned to his chair. She could tell he knew how moved she was at finally hearing her father talk about the battle. Jim reached for her hand and squeezed it. No words were needed.

***

Meanwhile, in the kitchen house, Jane and her grandmother were busy making molasses cookies. Jane was standing on a stool so she could reach the top of the table. Margaret let her dip out three scoops of flour and put it in the earthen bowl. She had traded a piece of lace she had tatted with a woman of the Catawba Nation for the piece of pottery.

"I'll add the spices," Margaret said. "These are precious, so we don't want to use too much."

"You've called me 'Precious' before, Grandma. "Am I as precious like your spices?

Margaret bent down to look Jane straight in the eyes. "No, Jane. You're much more precious than these spices."

Jane grinned. "What are they called?"

"This one is cinnamon." Margaret held it for Jane to smell it, then she sprinkled some on top of the flour and sugar. "And this is nutmeg."

"That's strong!" Jane said. She watched Margaret add a little to the bowl.

"This is ginger," Margaret said, holding it toward Jane's nose.

Jane's eyes lit up as she sniffed the fine powder before Margaret added it to the bowl.

"What's your favorite?" Margaret asked.

"Cinnamon."

"Mine, too. Take the spoon and gently mix all the dry ingredients together for me.

Jane grasped the wooden spoon with both hands and began to stir. "What else goes in the cookies?"

"An egg, some butter, honey, and molasses. I'll get them together while you stir."

Jane was careful to mix all the dry ingredients without letting much fly out of the bowl.

Margaret returned to the table balancing an egg, a lump of butter, and jars of honey and molasses in her hands. "Make a well," she instructed Jane. "You know what a well is, don't you?"

"Of course," Jane said. "It's a ditch in the flour."

"Your mother is teaching you well."

"Yes, she is," Jane said with conviction.

Margaret cracked the brown egg into the bowl, then added some honey and molasses. Jane stuck her finger out under the stream of honey and licked her finger and smacked her lips. "May I stir?" Jane asked.

"This is a stiff dough," Margaret said. "I'd better do it. I'm not sure you're strong enough. You have to hold the bowl up against your stomach while you stir it. Otherwise, the bowl might fall off the table and break."

Jane stood on tiptoe on her stool and watched Margaret mix the ingredients. "Did you get that spoon from the Catawba woman?"

"No. Your grandpa carved it. His skill and my using it every day for many years has made it smooth. I've made many puddings, pots of cornmeal mush, and batches of bread with this spoon."

"Do you think Grandpa could make me a spoon?"

"He might, if you ask him real nice. My arm is tired. I think the dough is mixed enough. You can take this smaller spoon and drop dough onto this tin pan."

Jane tried to drop lumps of dough onto the pan without getting the globs too close together.

"I see you've done this before," Margaret said. "You're doing a good job."

"Thank you," Jane said. "I've done it lots of times with you, Grandma, and sometimes with Mama."

When all the dough was finally on the pan, Margaret slid it into the brick-lined oven at the end of the chimney. "Won't be long now!"

Seeing her grandmother wipe her forehead with the back of her hand, Jane did the same thing. "It's hot in here," Jane said.

"That's what a bed of hot coals in this large fireplace will do," Margaret said. She fanned her face with the skirt of her apron and let out a tired sigh. "Your grandpa and your mama's first mother anticipated having a large family to feed. They built this fine kitchen house and gave it a massive fireplace."

"It's so tall, I could stand up in it, and I could lie down in it – if it was empty and clean – and stretch my arms up over my head and still have room left over!" Jane said. She stretched to demonstrate.

"That's true."

"How much longer till the cookies are ready?" Jane asked.

"I expect they're ready now." Margaret opened the iron latch on the stone oven. She took the pan of cookies out and put it on the table. "Careful, it's hot," she cautioned Jane.

"They sure smell good."

"They do. Let's get out a plate to put them on when they're cool. How would you like to serve them to Grandpa and your parents?"

"I'd like that."

***

When Jane and Margaret returned to the sitting room, John had dozed off. Grace and Jim were talking quietly. Jane stood in front of John's rocking chair with the plate of cookies. She scrunched up her face and looked at her mother. "Can I wake him up?" she whispered.

"Go ahead," Grace said. "He won't mind."

"Grandpa," Jane said. Nothing happened. "Grandpa," she said a little louder. "Grandpa!" That time John jumped, eyes wide open. "You were asleep."

"Just resting my eyes," John said.

"No, Grandpa. You were asleep."

"So I was," John said. "What were you and Grandma up to in the kitchen house all that time? You were gone a long time. Were you roasting a chicken?"

"No," Jane said. She giggled so hard she almost dropped the plate of cookies. "We made molasses cookies. Want one?"

"Don't mind if I do – if I can only have one."

Jane quickly counted the cookies, then counted the people in the room. "You can only have one. There are just enough."

John took a cookie and held it until Jane had given a cookie to each person. After she took the last cookie, Margaret took the plate and placed it on John's desk in the corner of the room. Everyone bragged on Jane's cookies and asked her if she'd made them all by herself. That made her blush. "No, Grandma helped me."

"I hope she'll give you the recipe, so you can make them at our house," Jim said.

Jane looked at her grandmother. "I can do that," Margaret said.

There was a momentary lull in the conversation, but it didn't take long for Jane to remember that her grandpa was getting ready to tell her a story when Grandma needed her in the kitchen house. "Grandpa, can you tell me that story now?"

"I'll be glad to," John said.

Jane crawled up on John's lap and snuggled under his lap blanket. He asked Jane where she wanted him to start.

"At the beginning."

"In the beginning, there was God," John said.

"No, Grandpa, not that beginning."

"In the beginning, our family came from County Tyrone in Ireland, but I was born in Virginia."

"Not that beginning!" Jane giggled. "The beginning of the rev—reva--"

"Revolution," Grace said. "That'll be a long story. We must get home before dark. Papa, just start with Kings Mountain."

"I was building up to that," John said. He winked at Jane. "We knew what we were doing, didn't we?"

"Yes, Grandpa. You like to tease me."

"During the Revolution, not everybody in the colonies wanted us to be free from Britain. Those of us who wanted freedom were called 'Patriots,' and those who did not were called 'Tories.'"

"One Saturday morning back in October of '80, a bunch of Tories up and camped out down near the smokehouse. They built themselves a big ol' fire and my papa figured they were going to kill one of our hogs. Papa grabbed his hunting rifle and was going to go see about it, but before he'd even gotten down the porch steps he heard shooting over toward the mountain."

"Kings Mountain?" Jane asked.

"That's right."

"Hearing the shooting, the Tories up and ran. Papa hurried back inside this very room and called for your great-uncle William to get his musket and go with him."

"What about Uncle James?" Jane asked.

"Your great-uncle James had been wounded in the war. He was home on furlough for six months until he could walk again."

"What about you, Grandpa? Get to the part about you and your mama. That's my favorite part of the story." Jane gave her parents a coy smile.

"I was in my sixteenth year – fifteen years old. I grabbed my rifle and ran out the door after Papa and William. I got to the edge of the woods out there and stopped. I started thinking maybe it wasn't a good idea for me to go. I looked back around toward the house, trying to make up my mind what to do. Mama was standing in the door. She yelled, "Go on and fight for your country, Johnny! Go on!"

Jane clapped her hands.

"That's my story," John said.

"No, it's not," Jane said. "Finish it. Please?"

"Mama telling me to go was all I needed. She gave me the courage to keep going and chase after Papa and William. We got over to the mountain... and whipped those Tories. The fight lasted little more than an hour, but the Patriots whipped the Tories, so we did."

"Yea!" Jane squealed and clapped her hands. "We won! We won!"

"Yes," John said. "We won. And now we don't have to do what a king across the ocean says. We live in a free and independent country."

"It's a shame none of you got recognized for what you did that day," Jim said.

"Yeah, we weren't in any organized group that took part in the battle, so you won't find our names on any list, but we did not do it for glory and for getting credit," John said. "We were fighting for our country and our neighbors and our family. I'm so glad Mama made me go to the battle. I have no regrets about that day. We were lucky to all come home unhurt. William went on and fought in the Battle of Guilford Courthouse. He did our family proud."

"I like that story," Jane said.

"Have I ever sung the song for you?" John asked.

"What song?" Jane asked.

"There's a song about the Battle of Kings Mountain," John said. "I remember part of it. It has a dozen verses, but I can't remember all the words. I think I can sing the first three verses."

John sang the first three verses of the ballad.

Jane clapped her hands. "I want to learn that song, but I don't know all those names."

"I'll help you learn it," Grace said. "I remember hearing it a lot when I was a little girl. It seemed like anytime there was a public gathering, everyone would sing that song. You need to learn it, so it will keep going for generations."

"What's a generation?" Jane asked.

"We'll explain that to you on the way home," Jim said. "We need to get going so we can get home before dark. Did you thank Grandpa for the story?"

"Thank you, Grandpa," Jane said. She reached up and hugged his neck. Her face rubbing up against his whiskers brought on another fit of giggles.

"We'll do it again next time you come for a visit," he said. "Eventually, you'll be able to tell the story and sing the song with me."

Jane grinned. "Maybe. And thank you for letting me help you make cookies, Grandma." She climbed down from John's lap and hugged Margaret.

"We'll do that again sometime, too," Margaret said. "I like having help in the kitchen. Your grandpa isn't much of a cook." Margaret winked at Jane.

Jane, Grace, and Jim said their goodbyes and bundled up against the cold. Jane skipped to their wagon and waited for her papa to boost her up onto the seat. Sitting between her parents, she looked over her shoulder until she could no longer see the two tall stone chimneys of her grandparents' log house.

Author's Note:

Kings Mountain rises some 800 feet above the surrounding terrain. In geological parlance, Kings Mountain and Crowders Mountain are monadnocks in the southern piedmont along the North Carolina-South Carolina border just a few miles west of Charlotte.

Monadnock is a term for an isolated small rock hill, mountain, or ridge that surprises you because there are no other mountains in sight. Kings Mountain and Crowders Mountain are not even in the foothills of the Appalachian Mountains chain. The surrounding area is gently rolling hills filled with oak, hickory, ash, pine, and dogwood trees.

Clarks Fork of Bullock's Creek is the name of the creek that runs through what used to be the McElwees' land. Its water eventually flows into the Catawba River. It is a beautiful area. The two mountains and surrounding state and federal parks are popular destinations for hikers and history buffs.

It is there that this story is set in 1823 and where the Battle of Kings Mountain took place in 1781 near the end of the American Revolutionary War.

The characters in the story hold a special place in my heart. Jane was my great-great-grandmother. Therefore, Grace and Jim were my great-great-great-grandparents, John Calvin McEwee was my great-great-great-great-grandfather, and John's second wife Margaret was my step-great-great-great-great-grandmother. John's first wife, Jane Leslie, was Grace's birth mother and the little girl in the story was named for her.

John Calvin McElwee; his brother, William McElwee III; and their father, William McElwee II, all fought in the Battle of King's Mountain on October 17, 1780. They were not members of any of the armed forces that took part in the battle, so their names do not show up on most lists of combatants. They are listed among the scores of local "Men who were possibly on the Kings Mountain Campaign or were possibly in the battle" in *The Patriots at Kings Mountain*, by Bobby Gilmer Moss. That book lists John McElwee (whose middle name was Calvin), James McElwee (John's brother), William McElwee, William McElwee II, and William McElwee III.

They participated in the battle because it took place less than two miles from their home near the North Carolina-South Carolina state line. Their service and the circumstances thereof are included in *Genealogy of William McElwee II of Clarks Fork of Bullocks Creek of York County, South Carolina*, compiled by Col. Pinckney Glasgow McElwee in 1959. In addition, there are family references on pages 421, 429, and 454 in the highly-respected book, *The Pictorial Field-Book of the Revolution, Vol 2*, by Benson J. Lossing, published 1859.

In fact, Mr. Lossing interviewed 87-year-old William McElwee III (brother of John Calvin McElwee) at his home in January 1849, when he was traveling the east coast and compiling his landmark book about locations that were important in the Revolutionary War. It was on that occasion that William McElwee III sang a portion of the ballad about the Battle of Kings Mountain for Mr. Lossing. I wanted to include those three verses from Lossing's book, but I was unable to determine if the song is now in the public domain.

The footnote in Lossing's book reads as follows: "The song called, "The Battle of King's Mountain," from which these lines are taken, was very popular in the Carolinas until some years after the close of the war. It was sung with applause at political meetings, wedding parties, and other gatherings, where the ballad formed a part of the proceedings. Mr. M'Elwees, on old man of eighty-seven, who fought under Sumter, and with whom I passed an evening, within two miles of King's Mountain, remembered it well, and repeated the portion here given."

I purchased a used copy of Lossing's book a few years ago. If you can find it, I highly recommend it to anyone interested in reading about what the land looked like in the 1840s and some of the first-hand accounts Lossing heard about the Amercian Revolutionary War.

I wanted to include all twelve verses of the ballad called "Ferguson's Defeat – 1780," which I found in an old used book, *Commanders at Kings Mountain*, by Rev. J.D. Bailey. The book was published in 1926 by Ed. H. DeCamp, Publishers, Gaffney, S.C. When I bought it, I didn't know if it would be of any use to me in my research and writing, but I took a chance on it. The words are the same as those attributed to "The Battle of King's Mountain" ballad quoted by Lossing. Again, since I was unable to determine without a doubt that the song was in the public domain without spending more time and money than I wanted to, the lyrics are not in my book. In his book, Rev. Bailey gives credit for the lyrics' inclusion to Dr. J.H. Logan, who found the ballad in the papers of Revolutionary War soldier Robert Long of Laurens, South Carolina. The songwriter's name is unknown.

I included a reference to the hanging of the ten Tories on the tulip tree after reading about that in a footnote Mr. Lossing included on page 423 of *The Pictorial Field-Book of the Revolution, Vol 2*, by Benson J. Lossing, 1859. It was a poplar tree that was brought to Mr. Lossing's attention when he visited Kings Mountain.

William McElwee II was born in County Tyrone, Ireland about 1718. He was a weaver. He boarded a ship for Philadelphia in 1750. In 1757 he married Janet Black in Pennsylvania. They soon moved to present-day Greenville County, Virginia, where their first three children, James, William III, and John Calvin McElwee were born.

While John was still a baby, the family moved to Clarks' Fork of Bullock Creek in North Carolina where William II received a grant of 200 acres of land on both sides of the creek in 1765. In 1772, surrounded by a great deal of confusion, the North Carolina/Suth Carolina boundary was established and overnight William McElwee II's land was no longer in North Carolina. It was in South Carolina.

The McElwees' two-story log house with two tall stone chimneys with massive fireplaces was torn down about 1934 after the land was acquired by the U.S. Government for the Kings Mountain National Military Park. According to Col. Pinckney Glasgow McElwee's family genealogy book, the foundation was still visible in 1959. As of 2025, my sister and I have not found anyone at the Kings Mountain National Military Park or the Kings Mountain State Park in South Carolina who can pinpoint the location of the McElwee house.

Originally covering 10,000 acres, more than half of the area of the federal park was transferred to the state of South Carolina for the state to develop an adjoining park. Although I have not been able to find the exact location of my McElwee ancestors' house, I have seen two photographs of it and the U.S. Department of the Interior had a draftsman measure and draw the house in detail. The photographs can be found on the website of the Library of Congress at https://www.loc.gov/item/sc0324/. The photographs as well as the elevation and floor plan drawings can be found at https://www.rootsandrecall.com/york-county-sc/buildings/william-mcelwee-house/?hilite=William+McElwee+Hou. I hope the drawings and photographs will continue to be available on the internet.

The McElwees were members of Bethany Associate Reformed Presbyterian Church near Clover, South Carolina, and many in the family's early generations are buried in the church cemetery, including William McElwee II and his wife, Janet Black McElwee as well as John Calvin McElwee and his first wife, Jane Leslie/Lessley McElwee and his second wife, Margaret.

The rest of the story is fiction. I do not know exactly what Jane Leslie McElwee said to her son, John Calvin McElwee, that convinced the

15-year-old to turn around and join in the battle, but the McElwee genealogy by Col. Pinckney Glasgow McElwee tells of that event.

I could have created a lot of conflict to make the story more exciting and captivating, but I chose not to embellish the lives of my ancestors in that way. I hope you enjoyed the story nevertheless.

A Letter from Sharpsburg

Author's Note:

The following letter is a fictional one that could have been written by a Confederate soldier who fought in the Battle of Sharpsburg. In the South, it was referred to as the Battle of Sharpsburg because that was the closest town to where the battle took place. In the North, it was referred to as the Battle of Antietam because that was the name of the creek there. (It was general practice in the Confederate States to refer to battles in the Civil War as the name of the nearest town, while the Union usually referred to battles using the name of a physical feature. Another example is the First and Second Battles of Bull Run (Union name) and the First and Second Battles of Manasses (Confederate name.)

I drew not only from historical accounts of the battle but also from letters that my great-grandfather, William Leroy Morrison, wrote to his parents and sister during the Civil War, although he did not fight in this battle in Maryland.

I chose to write this letter because more Americans were killed in this battle on September 17, 1862, than on any other day in United States military history. It is said that 2,100 Union soldiers and 1,550 Confederate soldiers were killed that day, with 9,550 Union soldiers and 7,750 Confederate soldiers being wounded.

This fictional letter is longer than a real letter from a Confederate soldier would have been. Paper for letter writing and postage stamps were usually scarce.

Saturday, September 20, 1862

Dear Mama and Papa,

I seat myself and take pen in hand to write you a few lines. Things have gone from bad to worse with me and our company since the last time I wrote. Don't feel hard toward me for not writing more letters. Camp is a terrible place to try to write. Some days we march all day. When we stop in the evening, I fall asleep. Other days there is nothing to do and I can't think of anything worth writing. Stamps are hard to come by.

General Lee has marched us across Maryland. With so many people here still undecided as to where their allegiance falls – North or South – General Lee thought we might help persuade folk if we sang "Maryland, My Maryland," as we marched. I'm telling you, if I never hear that song again, it will be too soon. Besides, I don't think it helped. Not that I would claim to know better than General Lee, but most folk stayed in their houses as we marched by.

Last Wednesday we saw the worst fighting I've seen since this war started. We were camped outside of a town in Maryland called Sharpsburg. On the other side of Antietam Creek was the Yankee army. They say there were 40,000 of us and 75,000 of them, but that might not be right. All I know is, we were terribly out-numbered.

It had rained the night before. The fog was just lifting that morning at daylight when the battle started. I'll never forget how the sun reflected off the Yankees' bayonets and rifles. It was a sight I don't wish to see again. We met the enemy head on in a corn field near a church of the German Baptists sect called Dunkers. I feel sorry for that farmer now because his corn field is soaked in the blood of Yankees and Confederates and his corn is flat on the ground.

It was as though the enemy soldiers were mad with the fever of battle. I couldn't hear anything except the shots of rifles and artillery fire, but it appeared to those of us who survived that the Yankees were laughing as they charged across the field at us. Boys fell to my left and to my right.

General Jackson sent in some reinforcements – boys from Texas -- to help us out. They were really mad because they'd been promised breakfast and didn't get any. Like us, they hadn't eaten in several days. Rations went from being short to none at all here lately.

The fighting between the Texans and the Yankees was fierce. The battle raged back and forth across that corn field probably fifteen times. More than half the Texans died in that field.

Up in the morning, the battle started up along a sunken country road south of where we were. We could hear the fighting. I understand from a handful of survivors from the 30th North Carolina that we met up with yesterday that the little sunken road became a pit for the dead Confederates with bodies lying two and three deep.

The third part of the battle happened farther to the south of our location at a stone bridge over Antietam Creek. After a hard-fought battle, the Yankees pushed across the bridge and the out-numbered Georgians in the fight retreated toward Sharpsburg. Just as things looked the darkest for the Confederacy, A.P. Hill arrived with his 3,000 troops. The funny thing about it, looking back on it, is that many of them were wearing blue uniforms they had taken from the Yankees they had killed in Harpers Ferry. The Yankees mistook them for Yankees and didn't fire on them until it was too late.

Night fell on the longest day of my life, and the fighting died with the daylight. I don't know yet how many men died or fell wounded last Wednesday, but it was the bloodiest day of fighting I ever hope to see. It was by far the worst day of my life. I hope I can live long enough to forget some of the things I saw on that day, but I fear it is not possible. The gruesome scenes of cruel war are printed on my memory forever. I cannot escape them, for it is as though they are painted on the inside of my eyelids. I close my eyes at night, but it is of no use. I cannot escape the horrors of last Wednesday, and I doubt I ever will.

By the time you have this letter in hand, you will probably already know that Cousin Joe died that day. Tell Aunt Mary we gave him a good Christian burial, the best we could. Tom and Jim were killed in the battle. So were William, Charlie, and Leroy. That's just the ones from our little school at home. There were many others in our company that never made it off that corn field -- Frank, Oliver, and Zeke. I never thought I would lose so many good friends and neighbors in one day.

There's no easy way to tell you this, Mama, but a bullet grazed my left arm. There were so many wounded – most of them worse than me -- that they had to get to us as they could. I bandaged my arm best I could until a doctor looked at it yesterday. He said I will be all right. After what I saw in battle, I'll take my grazing and thank the Lord for it.

Tell Sis that I will write her a letter soon. Her ears are too young to hear the words in this letter. Tell her that I am well. Tell her to eat some pears for me, but not too many at one time. I hope there is a good crop of them this year.

In your last letter you asked me what I needed. We need anything you could send, but I don't know where our company will be. We're back in Virginia now. Our clothes are all in tatters. My britches are patched in the seat, but so are everyone else's. My shoes are worn out. We are a sorry looking bunch. I use what little money I have to buy food when we are in friendly territory.

Try not to worry about me. I left home a boy of 17, but I shall, the Lord willing, return to you a man.

Your obedient son until death,

John

Questions for your consideration:

(1) John knew that his parents would know the other boys and young men from his company who were killed that day at Antietam/Sharpsburg. Why did men from the same communities serve together in military companies during the Civil War, and why did this practice eventually cease to be permitted in the United States military (an exception being the National Guard today)?

(2) It has been said by some historians that if Confederate reinforcements had not arrived, the United States Army might have beaten the Confederate Army so severely at Antietam/Sharpsburg that the Civil War might have ended then and not dragged on for nearly three more years. How do you think that would have influenced long-term hard feelings between people from The North and people from The South? Would the nation have healed more quickly if the Civil War had not lasted for four years?

Bibliography for "Letter from Sharpsburg"

Burns, Ken; Burns, Ric; and Ward, Geoffrey C. *The Civil War: An Illustrated History*. New York: Alfred A. Knopf, Inc., 1990.

Fuller, Major General J.F.C. *Grant and Lee: A Study in Personality and Generalship*. Bloomington, Indiana: Indiana University Press, 1957.

Lossing, Benson J. *Pictorial Field Book of the Civil War: Journeys Through the Battlefields in the Wake of Conflict*. Vol. II: *Reorganizing the Army of the Potomac to the Capture of Vicksburg*. Baltimore: The Johns Hopkins University Press, 1997. (Originally published by T. Belknap in 1876.)

Morrison, William Leroy. Photocopies of parts of letters written to his parents and sister while serving in the army of the Confederate States of America, 1864.

Woodhead, Henry, ed. *Echoes of Glory: Illustrated Atlas of the Civil War*. Alexandria, Virginia: Time-Life Books, 1998.

http://www.nps.gov/anti/

http://www.civilwarhome.com/antietam.htm

SLIP SLIDING AWAY

Southern Appalachian Mountains
1875

It was what you might call a hard place to keep a secret. Strangers were warned, "Don't say anything bad about anybody here. Everybody's kin to everybody."

The fire crackled and hissed as the flames danced and uncovered hidden pockets of sap in the logs in the Johnsons' fireplace. Melted snowflakes sizzled as they fell down the stone chimney. The late March wind howled. It had been snowing off and on for three days.

Such a late spring snowstorm was not unheard of, but it was not commonplace. There had not been a blizzard this late in the spring in any of the six years the Johnsons had lived in this southern Appalachians cove. Everyone was staying close to home. Farm work had to be done, such as feeding and watering the horses and livestock, but most folks were just trying to stay warm.

Hannah Johnson blew a series of long, hot breaths on the windowpane and then rubbed a small area of the glass in vigorous circular motions with the hem of her blue wool shawl. Her efforts to clear a peephole in the one-room log cabin's lone window were all for naught.

Although the inside of the window was just glazed over with frost, the outside was covered in a sheet of ice.

Several days earlier, Hannah had found the intricate patch of white frost on her window to be interesting. But as the days dragged on and the cold and snow were unrelenting, she had begun to worry that her sister would not be able to come perform her midwife duties if her time came before the thaw began.

Hannah's husband, Daniel, had strained himself severely a few days ago and had taken to bed. The moving of the log he was working with would have been a difficult task for two strong men, so Hannah had scolded him for not seeking help from her brother or one of his brothers who all lived nearby. Daniel was the eldest, then there were James, Frank, Thomas, and Billy. Any one of them would have helped Daniel if they had just known what he was doing that day. As a result of his foolishness, Daniel now lay in the bed in great pain.

The closeness of the frosty window and the air seeping in around its loose frame sent a shiver through Hannah's body. She tugged at her shawl and pulled it more tightly around her neck and shoulders. She walked over to the corner cupboard where she kept her most prized possessions and reached for a small wooden box on the top shelf. Daniel was not even allowed to open this box. It was Hannah's private repository of treasures. It held her mother's wedding band, the lace-trimmed handkerchief Hannah had carried on her wedding day, a piece of paper on which an old beau had written a poem, and a small, yellowed, paper handmade envelope.

Hannah removed the envelope from the box and squinted in the dim firelight to see how much of the rich, fine, powdery contents remained. She poured a cup of hot tea for Daniel at the hearth and carefully sprinkled some of the powder into it. She slipped the envelope into her skirt pocket so it would be handy if Daniel needed an additional dose.

Daniel moaned and tried to shift his position in the bed as Hannah approached. "Here, take some tea, Daniel," she said softly as she sat down in the rocking chair beside the bed. The tea had a soothing affect and seemed to make his sleep more restful. Though the cabin was impossible to heat during such cold and windy weather, Daniel's forehead glistened with sweat which trickled down his temples and wet his hair. Hannah gently dabbed at the beads of sweat on Daniel's red and burning face while shivering in the drafty cabin. She made a mental note to ask her brother-in-law, James, to replace the missing mud chinks between the logs in the wall before the next winter.

"Tick... tock... tick.... tock...." The steady ticking of the mantel clock nearly lulled Hannah to sleep and caused her to daydream. As she sat and looked at Daniel, she could not help but think about his brother, James. The two men were nothing alike in looks or personality. Whereas Daniel had a roughness about him, James had a gentleness that she had been drawn to since they were children growing up in Ireland.

Things could have been so different if that Sarah McEwen had not come along when we were fourteen and the boys were starting to show an interest! Sarah came to Carrickfergus with her Scottish accent. She was new and exciting and turned all the lads' heads. This could have been James' baby, she thought as she rubbed her hands over her round abdomen. *And those could have been James' sons playing there by the hearth.*

Hannah straightened her tired back and heard several stiff bones in her spine and neck pop and crackle. Her mind turned to the spring planting. *Here we are getting the coldest weather of the season just when the farmers are getting ready to put in their new crops. Now it will be weeks before it's dry enough to plow. I should have already planted mustard greens, kale, cabbage, lettuce, and turnips in my spring garden. With the baby coming soon, how will I ever get my garden in?* Suddenly, the clock struck eight.

"It's time for bed," Hannah said to her two sons, five-year-old Will and three-year-old Ben. "Get in the bed and I will listen to you say your prayers."

The boys raced to see who could get under the covers first. Hannah had devised this game to encourage her two reluctant boys to go to bed. She helped them with the covers, which consisted of three quilts her sister and sisters-in-law had helped her make. One was of the log cabin design, while the other two were crazy quilts. Log cabin was her favorite quilt pattern, so she always kept it on top where she could enjoy seeing it. She smiled at her two young sons and sat down on the edge of the feather bed they shared.

"Dear God, please help my papa feel better," Will prayed. "He needs to get well so he can work the farm and raise our food like he did last summer." Hannah swallowed hard.

"Dear God, thank you for the snow," Ben added. Hannah cringed, but kept her eyes closed.

"Dear God, thank you for Will and Ben. Keep them safe throughout the night," Hannah prayed.

"And bless them in the morning light," Will finished his mother's nightly prayer.

"And don't let the bed bugs bite!" Ben added.

"Amen," the three of them said together. Hannah tucked the three layers of quilts snugly under her sons' chins and kissed each one good-night on the forehead.

With the boys asleep a few minutes later, Hannah sat down in the rocking chair beside her husband's bed and turned her attention back to him. He moaned in pain and he burned with fever. She held his head up with one hand and spoon fed him some tea with the other.

"They're coming to get us!" Daniel called out. He sat straight up in bed for a moment and then fell back with a thud.

"Who's coming to get us?" Will screamed. He and Ben scrambled out of bed and ran to their mother's open arms.

"No one's coming to get us," Hannah assured them. "He's having a nightmare is all. Go back to bed." She shooed the boys in the direction of their bed and let them tuck themselves in this time.

"They're coming in the door!" Daniel yelled.

Hannah jumped but tried to steady her voice. "You're having a nightmare. It's not real, Daniel. It's not real." She continued her vigil, dabbing sweat from his face and chest every few minutes. Just as she would drift off to sleep in her chair beside Daniel's bed, he would startle her with another outburst.

"They're coming! They're coming in the door now! Look! They're at the window! Don't let them in, Papa! Don't let them kill us! No! No!" There was pure terror in his voice. It was a nightmare Daniel endured every time he ran a high fever.

Daniel continued to call out in his sleep. By midnight Hannah was unable to rouse him. As the night went on, Daniel fell deeper into a fitful but quiet sleep. By three o'clock in the morning, his breathing had become irregular. At times many seconds passed between his breaths and Hannah would hold her own breath to see if her husband would make another effort to inhale.

At those times Hannah would sit on the edge of her chair, her eyes watching for a rise or fall in Daniel's chest. Her eyes and ears strained for any indication that he was still alive. Occasionally, Hannah would doze off to sleep, only to wake up with a start when her head fell forward or when Daniel took a deep breath.

The dark, gray dawn was scarcely distinguishable from the night as Daniel breathed his last. Hannah gasped, then waited for her husband to breathe again. After so many false alarms, she could not be sure. This time it had been too long. She waited a few more seconds. His chest did not rise or fall. She counted twenty ticks from the clock. There was not another breath.

"Daniel," Hannah whispered. There was no response. She did not want to awaken the boys, so she put her lips to Daniel's ear and shook him with both hands as she said his name again as loudly as she dared. There was still no response.

"Daniel!" she said once more as she gave his body another good shake. Hannah felt the blood drain from her face as her knees went weak. She let go of Daniel's shoulders in order to steady herself and sit down on the edge of the bed. The straw mattress and bed frame creaked under her weight.

Then the room was silent again except for her own breathing, the rhythmic ticking of the clock, and the occasional hissing of the glowing coals in the fireplace as they were hit by drops of melted snow or bits of sleet. Hannah stroked Daniel's hair, which was still wet with sweat, and her mind raced. There were things that needed to be taken care of before the boys woke up or word was sent to the neighbors.

Hannah methodically washed and prepared her husband's body for burial. She worked quickly but silently. She carefully shaved the stubble off Daniel's face and neck, dressed him in his best shirt, and combed his hair. She stood over his body for a minute to catch her breath and admire her work. *He cleaned up pretty well after all. And underneath that rough demeanor, he was still a handsome man. Well, not as handsome as James, but handsome enough.* There was a peace in Daniel's face that had not been there for several days.

Hannah took the basin of dirty water and rested it on her hip as she carefully opened the heavy oak door. She poured the water out beside the door. It had stopped snowing but was still windy and bitterly cold. She stepped back and closed the door as quickly and quietly as she could. She returned the basin to the washstand and poured into it the last of the water in the pitcher.

She splashed the cold water on her face and looked up to find a stranger's reflection in the mirror as she reached for a towel. Her long auburn hair was a mess and the dark circles under her eyes betrayed her exhaustion. *Is that a gray hair?* she wondered, fingering an unmistakable strand of silver at her left temple. *I have become an old woman!* She stared at her reflection in the mirror in disbelief. *I have become my own mother!* she gasped, almost out loud, as her hand flew to her mouth. *I must fix myself up. I can't have people see me like this. I can't let James see me like this!*

Tears almost came to Hannah's eyes as she brushed her hair which reached to her waist. Her hair brush had been a wedding gift from

Daniel. The handle and back were silverplate with an intricate Celtic design. Her fingers slowly traced the lines of the lovers' knot on the back of the brush as her mind traveled back to Ireland and their wedding day eight years ago. Daniel had spent much more than he should have on the brush. It seemed frivolous to Hannah, then and now, and typical of the way Daniel mishandled money. *He wasted money and here I sit wasting time*, she thought, and she put the brush down.

Hannah let her thick hair fall down her back. She reached behind her neck, and from memory her fingers quickly divided her hair into three equal bunches. Her fingers flew as she braided her hair. It was a routine she could have done in her sleep. She deftly arranged the single braid into a figure-eight on the back of her head. Just as she finished securing the last hairpin, there was a knock at the door. Will and Ben jumped up from a deep sleep.

"It's all right, lads. Go back to sleep. Coming!" Hannah called as she went to the door. Will and Ben were always slow to wake up, especially in the winter. They both squirmed, burrowed deeper under their covers, and squeezed their eyes shut to block out the morning light which swept across the room when Hannah opened the door.

Hannah could not hide her delight that it was Daniel's brother, James, at the door. James' wife, Sarah, had died in childbirth the summer before, leaving James all alone on the adjacent farm. He had been good to come and help Daniel with various farming chores. In return, Hannah had invited him to join them for many meals. There was an easy familiarity between the two of them now.

"Come in and try to get warm," Hannah said, ushering James inside. "I was just getting ready to build up the fire. I didn't mean to let it go completely out overnight. Let me hang up your coat." James removed his wet, wool coat and Hannah hung it on the back of a cane-bottomed chair by the hearth.

"I'll tend the fire for you," James said as he easily lifted a huge back log and laid it on the andirons at the rear of the deeply recessed stone fireplace. "You have no business trying to pick up these logs now. I'm glad I got here when I did."

"Me, too," Hannah said. She watched as James skillfully rearranged the embers and remaining bits of log left from the night's fire. He leaned down and blew into the glowing coals. They suddenly blazed and soon there was a roaring fire.

"Now, that's better!" James said as he brushed his hands together to knock off the dirt and residue from the logs.

"It certainly is!" Hannah said. "Whatever brings you out so early in this weather?"

"I knew Daniel was laid up and thought you could use some help with the animals. How is he?" James asked, turning to see Daniel's body. "Hannah!"

"He died about an hour ago," Hannah whispered, putting her right forefinger to her closed lips. "I haven't told Will and Ben yet. They're still asleep. They practically worshiped their father. I haven't prepared them for this kind of news."

James' eyes expressed his shock and his sympathy to Hannah. He grasped her hand, put his other arm around her shoulder, and gave her a reassuring hug. She responded to his touch by embracing him. They held each other tightly. James suddenly released her, as if he felt uncomfortable or embarrassed. It was an awkward moment. Hannah noticed that James' cheeks were flushed.

James cleared his throat and fumbled for words. "I'm sorry. I didn't mean to ...." His voice trailed off. He turned and walked to Daniel's bed. Hannah followed and stood beside him.

"Why didn't you tell me when I got here?" James asked. His eyes were rimmed with tears.

"I... I didn't know how to tell you," Hannah said. "I wasn't expecting you so early. I know how close you are... were to Daniel. He had a big influence on you after your father died."

"That's true, but you've lost *your* husband," James said.

"I have to be strong for the lads," she said.

"But the lads are asleep. You don't have to be so brave yet," James said.

"Well, maybe I could...." Hannah's voice broke and she nearly collapsed in a flood of tears. James caught her just in time. Putting nearly all her weight on James, she let him gently guide her into the rocking chair. He knelt at her feet and, sobbing, she buried her face in his chest.

After a couple of minutes, James started to pull away and Hannah sensed he was uneasy with their closeness. "I'll get you a glass of water," he said and he got some water for her with a gourd dipper in the oak bucket on the dining table. "Here, take a swig of water," he said as he handed the glass to Hannah. She felt his eyes on her as she drank half the water without stopping to breathe.

"Thank you," she said. "I suppose I needed to have a good cry before the lads woke up. I was trying to hold it all in."

"I know how it is to lose the love of your life, you know. You don't have to be brave in front of me," James said.

"You probably understand what I'm going through better than anyone else," Hannah said.

"Maybe so, but your situation is different. You're a woman with two small children and another on the way. It isn't going to be easy for you," James said.

"No, it won't be easy, but having you and the rest of the family close by will be a help. We'll make it through somehow," Hannah said, wiping her eyes and nose.

"I hate to bring it up," James said, clearing his throat, "but we'll need to have the funeral this evening. I'll go tell Frank and the others. I assume you want us brothers to be pallbearers," James said.

"Yes, of course. Thank you. And could one of you get word to the preacher?"

"You know I will. I'll go spread the word and come back to tend to the animals. Is there anything else you need me to do before I leave?"

"No. That's all. You go on. I have to gather my wits and tell Will and Ben about their father."

"Do you need me to stay and help you tell them?" James asked.

"No. You have several stops to make. I can do it."

With that, James gave Daniel's body another long look, nodded to Hannah, shrugged into his still wet coat, and headed for the door. He stopped with his hand on the latch and turned back to her. "I'll get Joseph Black to make the coffin, if that's agreeable with you," he said.

"Oh... yes. I hadn't even thought about the coffin. What would I do without you?" Hannah asked.

James gave a weak smile as he left. Another blast of cold air filled the room before he could get the door closed behind him. Hannah shivered and was nearly overcome with emotion. She pulled her shawl more tightly around her shoulders and stared in the direction of the door.

Oh, James, if you only knew! she thought to herself. *Now the way is clear for me to have you. I could tell by the way you touched me just now that you have feelings for me, too. And you love Will and Ben like they were your own, and now they will be your own. I've waited all my life for you! Now the waiting is almost over, but I have things I have to do today.*

Hannah collected her thoughts for a few minutes, took two handkerchiefs from the top drawer of the bureau, then sat down on the edge of Ben and Will's bed. Only the tops of their heads were showing from under the quilts. She pulled back the covers just a few inches and touched each of the boys on the shoulder. They wiggled and shivered, keeping their eyes tightly shut. Hannah spoke their names softly and rubbed their shoulders until they rolled over and slowly opened their eyes. They yawned and stretched. Feeling the cold air in their corner of the cabin, they quickly snuggled back under the covers.

"Wake up, lads," Hannah said and she firmly shook their shoulders. "I have something to tell you. You must wake up." They rubbed the sleep from their eyes and Hannah pulled the covers back ever so slightly so she could look them in the eye. She took a deep breath. She had never been one to sugarcoat bad news, not even for the children.

"I have something very sad to tell you," Hannah started. Will yawned and stretched while Ben rubbed the sleep from his half-shut eyes.

"What is it, Mother?" Will asked. "Is it Papa? Is he sicker?"

"It is about your Papa. He got very sick during the night. I did everything I knew to do, but he died. Your Papa is dead," she said.

"But he can't be dead! He's my Papa and he can't be dead," Will cried. "I want to see Papa! He's just asleep! Let me go!" he said, struggling against the firm grasp of his mother.

"Not yet, Will," Hannah said, and Will collapsed in sobs.

"Why is Will crying? What means 'dead'?" Ben asked.

"Do you remember last summer when that cardinal flew into the window and broke its neck?" Hannah asked.

"Yes. It didn't move. It didn't fly any more. Did Papa break his neck?" Ben asked.

"No, your Papa did not break his neck, but he was very, very sick. Like that little bird, your Papa can't move any more. He has gone to be with Jesus up in heaven," she explained.

"Papa won't be here to ever take us fishing again, Ben," Will said, straightening up and wiping the tears from his cheeks. "He's gone and he's never coming back! He's not ever coming back, is he Mother?"

Hannah handed him a handkerchief. "No, Will. He's never coming back."

Both boys sobbed uncontrollably and could not be consoled, Ben buried his face in his pillow. He and Will cried until they were too exhausted to cry. After a few minutes, Ben sat up and took the other handkerchief from his mother.

"Are you ready to see your Papa now?" Hannah asked. The boys nodded that they were.

Hannah took them by their hands and led them over to see their father. She didn't want them to be afraid of a dead body, so she encouraged them to touch his clothing and then to touch his hair. This they did and it seemed to calm them.

"Papa," Ben whispered. He repeated, "Papa!" a little louder. He leaned his face very close to that of his father and searched for any sign of life. Will joined him. "He could be asleep," Ben whispered to his brother. "What do you think?"

"I think he's dead. I don't hear him breathing," Will said.

Then, to Hannah's surprise, Ben reached up and touched his father's cheek. Then Will did the same thing. Hannah put her hand on Daniel's forehead and found it still warm from the fever. She was pleased at the ease with which her two young sons were accepting their father's body. She had thought this would be the most difficult part of the task, but then they started asking questions. Their young ears had picked up bits and pieces of Rev. Matthews' sermons.

"Are you going to die, too, Mother? Is Papa with Jesus now or did he go to that other place? The preacher says we must not take the name of the Lord in vain and Papa did that almost every day. Did Papa go to that bad place -- that fiery furnace the preacher talks about? Can we go where he is, except if he's in that fiery furnace I don't want to go there! I'm afraid of fire, Mother. When will we see Papa again? Can he come back to visit us? Can he see us? Will we be able to see him? Who is there with him? Is he lonesome? Will he get enough to eat, Mother? You know how he loves to eat!" There was an endless string of questions all morning.

Hannah's brother, John, and his wife, Margaret, arrived in time for Margaret to put the finishing touches on the stew Hannah was heating for lunch. Margaret had brought a loaf of bread she had baked that morning, figuring correctly that Hannah had not had time to bake any for the day.

"I feel so bad for you, Hannah. You're here with the two young lads and another bairn on the way. How are you going to manage? How are you going to keep the farm going?" Margaret asked.

"I suppose I will manage the best I can," Hannah replied.

"You surely are putting up a brave front. If something happened to John, I would be all to pieces," Margaret said.

"I guess I'm just not a very emotional person. Crying won't help the situation. I have to be strong for the boys. It wouldn't do for them to see their mother all upset, now would it?" Hannah responded, almost with a smile.

"I suppose not," Margaret said, but there was more than a hint of doubt in her voice. "The lads' eyes are red and swollen. I can tell they took it hard."

"Aye, but better than I thought they might," Hannah said. "They were full of questions."

While the two women chatted and prepared the table, John tried to entertain his two nephews with a gee-haw whimmy-diddle. The homemade wooden toy whirled like a top in John's skillful hands. He delighted in making the boys laugh.

"Come to the table," Hannah called to John and the boys.

They all took seats around the sturdy oak table Daniel had made. They bowed their heads and John said grace.

"I'm not hungry," Ben said.

"We all need to eat. We have a long afternoon ahead of us," Hannah said.

"Why is the afternoon going to be long?" Ben asked.

"We have to go to the church for your father's burial. With all the ice and snow on the ground, it will take us longer to get there than usual. It is very cold. You will have to bundle up in all your warm clothes," Hannah said.

Just as they were finishing their lunch, Daniel's four brothers and two neighbors arrived with a pine coffin to collect his body. That morning they'd dug a grave in the frozen soil on top of that windy hill where the church sat. It had been a difficult day for them physically and emotionally, and it was not over yet.

"Whew! I can tell you have already been into the burial liquor!" Hannah said, waving her hand in front of her face as soon as the men entered the house. "I do hope you aren't drunk!"

"Naw, we ain't drunk, Miss Hannah," one of the neighbors said.

"You smell to high heaven! You aren't fooling me," Hannah said. "Please don't do anything to embarrass me this afternoon."

"We won't," Daniel's brother, James, said. "Some of us can hold our liquor better than others. You know it's tradition."

"Why else would they call it burial liquor?" Daniel's brother, Frank, asked. "It's like James said. It's just tradition. Daniel would want us to enjoy some whiskey before his funeral. And besides, it's awful cold out there. We had to fortify ourselves."

Hannah glared at the six men one at a time, then spoke. "I suppose you want to see the body. You'll hardly know him. He cleaned up real good."

The six pallbearers all stood, hats in hand, staring at Daniel's body. No one spoke for a few minutes. Finally, one-by-one, they commented to Hannah about how good Daniel looked.

"He sure does look natural," Daniel's brother, Thomas, said, though nothing could be further from the truth. There were nods of agreement all around although the last time Daniel had worn a proper suit of clothes was on his wedding day. He was hardly recognizable, clean-shaven and all dressed up.

After there was nothing else to be said, James cleared his throat. "We'd better be getting a move on, boys. Hannah, are you ready for us to... to put him... to put Daniel's body... in the coffin?"

"Yes. I'm ready," Hannah said. Will and Ben clung to her and fought back tears. They were trying to be brave in front of their uncles. They were frightened and curious at the same time. They'd never seen a dead body before and needed to watch to learn how such things were handled.

Will looked up at his mother's face. "Why aren't you crying, Mother?" he asked.

"Everyone handles grief in their own way, lad," she answered, never looking at him as the men lifted Daniel's body into the coffin. She and the boys watched as James took some nails out of his pocket, reached for his hammer, and nailed the lid shut.

"That's it, I guess," James said to no one in particular. "Let's get on with it."

Hannah opened the door and she and her sons stepped outside and watched as the coffin was carried out of the cabin and loaded into James' wagon for the arduous trip to the graveyard at the church. The snow-covered terrain was hilly and there were two creeks to ford. James and Billy climbed up into the wagon seat, while the other four men got on their horses. Hannah thanked them and hurried back inside the cabin to get herself and her two sons ready to go to the funeral.

***

All along the way, the pallbearers reminisced about their departed brother and friend and heartily tried to drown their sorrows in the whiskey Frank had provided. They agreed that it would be a good idea to stop at Billy's house and warm themselves by the fire before beginning the final segment of their journey. It was difficult for them to leave the cozy confines of Billy's cabin, especially after Billy brought out another jug of whiskey. They stayed on longer than they had intended, but eventually forced themselves back out into the the cold.

"There goes John's wagon and Hannah and the boys," James said as two wagons passed Billy's house. "We shouldn't have stayed here so long. Come on, boys! Let's get a move on! We still have to cross Antlers Creek and get up that last hill."

"Whose idea was it to build the church on a hill anyway?" one of the pallbearers asked.

"I guess they were afraid of a flood or something," James speculated.

"I reckon so, but couldn't they at least have put the graveyard at the bottom of the hill?" another one added. There were laughs of agreement all around.

The horses struggled to pull the wagon through the half-frozen creek. James gave the beasts verbal encouragement and a few swats on their rumps. The four men on horseback were having problems of their own coaxing their animals up the steep hill in the deep snow after splashing through the icy water.

"We've just about made it," James said. "Try not to let on we're drunk."

***

"Here they come! I can see they're approaching the creek," Rev. Matthews announced to the mourners who were wrapped in blankets and waiting in their wagons in front of the church. They were dressed in their Sunday finery, all wearing hats and the women wore gloves and heavy wool capes.

John helped Hannah down from the wagon seat. She and the other women stepped gingerly through the icy snow, trying to keep their balance. John held Hannah's arm tightly and led her to the front of the procession. They walked behind the church where field stones and a few sheets of slate marked some 20 graves, mostly of children.

"Let us sing until they get here with the body," Rev. Matthews said as the dozen or so mourners gathered around the open grave.

***

As the strains of "Rock of Ages" drifted on the wind from the graveyard, the drunken pallbearers struggled to guide the wagon across the creek and up the hill. The horses strained against the cold and slippery ground.

"We've got a problem, y'all," Frank said.

"What do you mean, 'Try not to let on we're drunk?'" Thomas asked. "The wind is at our backs. They probably smelled us a mile away!"

"I think we have a problem here," Frank interrupted again.

"Quiet!" James said, not realizing how loudly he was talking. The singing stopped and heads turned to see what the commotion was all about.

"We definitely have a problem here, y'all." Frank was insistent but continued to be ignored.

"Keep quiet, I said!" James repeated. "We just have to get up this hill and we'll be there."

The wagon and ragtag procession of pallbearers continued up the hill to the graveyard. "Rock of Ages" got louder and sounded worse, the closer they got.

James set the brake on the wagon and he and Billy climbed down from the seat. The other four pallbearers more or less slid off their horses and mustered all the decorum they could. Their hats were askew and their trousers were splattered with mud. James looked around at the other pallbearers and shook his head.

The singing gradually stopped as the mourners all turned their heads toward the pallbearers. Some stopped in mid-word, their mouths open.

"At least tuck in your shirt tails!" James said in a low but disgusted voice. "Hannah asked us not to embarrass her!" The men looked down at themselves, some scratching their heads. Others spit in the snow. Most eventually made feeble attempts to make themselves more presentable.

Several uneasy minutes passed while everyone waited for the pallbearers to bring the coffin from the wagon. Hannah tried to hide her embarrassment that her husband's pallbearers -- his brothers and closest friends -- had arrived at his funeral so intoxicated with burial liquor that they could hardly stand. They had started out earlier in the afternoon in their Sunday-best clothing, but all stood in tatters now.

Rev. Matthews cleared his throat and nodded to James, Frank, and the other pallbearers, but none of them moved or spoke. The wind picked up and the graveside mourners shivered in the cold. All eyes rested on the silent pallbearers.

Trying not to move his lips or speak too loudly, Frank repeated, "We have a problem, James. We've lost—"

"Gentlemen," Rev. Matthews interrupted, his voice cracking in disbelief that he had chosen to address the group with such a misnomer. "Please bring the body," he continued, and with a sweep of his hand he indicated where the coffin should be placed.

"Oh. Ah... of course," James stammered. "Come on, y'all. Give me a hand," he said. The others fell in line behind him and they walked to the back of the wagon. James untied the canvas cover and pulled it back.

"Well I'll be—!" James exclaimed.

One-by-one, four of the other men chimed in with various expressions of disbelief at what they saw or, more accurately, what they did not see.

"Where's the coffin?" James demanded, trying to keep his voice down so the people gathered around the grave would not hear.

"That's what I've been trying to tell you!" Frank whispered. "Daniel is gone!"

"What do you mean he's gone? A body doesn't just get up and walk off!" James whispered.

"Is there a problem, gentlemen?" Rev. Matthews called out.

James turned and smiled at the pastor. "Just a minute, preacher. We'll be with you in just a minute." He tried to sound reassuring and offered another little smile and tipped his hat before turning his back on the pastor and mourners.

"Why didn't you say something?" James demanded through gritted teeth, getting in Frank's stubbled face.

"Why didn't I say something? Why didn't I *say* something?" Frank's voice rose in disgust. "I've been trying to tell you all the way up the hill! Nobody ever listens to me!"

"What happened?" James asked. "And keep your voice down."

"All I know is I turned around and the coffin was gone," Frank said.

"When did it disappear?" James asked. "How did you let this happen?"

"*Let* it happen? You were the one driving the wagon!" Frank said.

"But you were supposed to be watching the coffin, Frank," James said.

"Yeah, that was the plan, but I got tired looking at that coffin. I wasn't expecting it to do anything, so I quit watching," Frank said.

"Just sing another hymn, folks. I'll go see what the hold up is," Rev. Matthews said and he started toward the wagon. "I've just about lost all my patience, boys. What in the world are you doing?" he asked in a low voice as he approached the wagon. All eyes fell on James, the most sober of the group. "Is there a problem?"

"Well, sort of, preacher," James answered.

"What do you mean, 'sort of?' It's freezing out here and will soon be dark! Let's get on with it!" Rev. Matthews said.

"We can't," Frank volunteered.

"Why not?" the minister asked, trying to keep his temper in check.

"Because... because we've lost Daniel," James said.

All the color drained from the pastor's face. He pushed his way to the wagon and looked in.

"Where is the body?" Rev. Matthews asked. His jaw was set.

"We don't rightly know, preacher," Frank said. "We know we started out with him. And we know we made it part of the way—"

"Where were you the last time you knew you had him?" Rev. Matthews interrupted.

"I know he was here when we stopped at Billy's house to... to—" Frank's voice trailed off.

"To warm ourselves," James said.

"I don't rightly remember seeing him after that," Frank said.

"If he was still in the wagon when we left Billy's but he's not in it now, that means he must have slid out while we were coming up the hill," James said.

"Or maybe when we were coming up out of the creek," Billy added.

"I'll stall for time and you fellows find Daniel and get his body back up here as fast as you can - and I mean hurry!" Rev. Matthews said. He slowly returned to the crowd gathered around the open grave. He looked grim, but tried to hide his concern and anger.

"There will be a short delay before the service can commence," Rev. Matthews said.

Hannah looked toward the pallbearers. "Where are they going?" she shrieked. "And why is the wagon empty? What have they done with Daniel?" Several mourners gasped and one woman fainted. Hannah erupted in gales of laughter which were initially misinterpreted as sobbing.

"There, there, Mrs. Johnson," Rev. Matthews said, stepping toward Hannah. "I know this is terribly upsetting, but ...." Then he realized she was laughing uncontrollably and not crying at all.

"You are hysterical, Mrs. Johnson!" he said. "You must stop this. You must get yourself pulled together!" Rev. Matthews took her by the shoulders and shook her. By now everyone was gaping at Hannah in disbelief. The woman who had fainted had been revived and taken back to her family's wagon.

"Oh, I'm sorry. How embarrassing," Hannah said, hiding her face with her handkerchief and trying to stop laughing. *Are they ever going to get Daniel buried?* she wondered.

"It's all right, Hannah," John said, trying to comfort his sister. "She'll be all right, folks," he said to the crowd. "She's just overcome with grief."

"We could take shelter in the church until they return, Mrs. Johnson," Rev. Matthews suggested.

"Yes," Hannah said. "That's sounds like a good idea. That would at least get us out of this wind." John took her by the arm to assist her through the snow that was at least twelve inches deep. It was deeper than that where the wind had blown it in drifts.

With Hannah, her children, and the other women in attendance safely seated inside the sanctuary, John stepped back outside to get some information from the minister.

"What is going on, Preacher?" John asked. The two men stood on the large flat stone which served as the only step leading into the church. "What happened to Daniel's body? What the … a … what's going on?"

"The best I could determine from talking to James and Frank, Daniel was in the wagon before they crossed Antlers Creek. My guess is that the coffin slid out of the wagon as they came out of the water and up the hill. In the men's efforts to get the wagon and their horses up the hill in this ice and snow, no one noticed the coffin falling out of the wagon," Rev. Matthews explained.

"Now if that don't beat all!" John said. "It appeared to me that the fools were all drunk as skunks, too! No wonder none of them noticed a little thing like a coffin with a man's body inside sliding out of the wagon! And it their own brother!" John said, shaking his head in disgust.

***

Meanwhile, the pallbearers got back down the hill to the creek. "There's the coffin," Thomas shouted, "standing straight up on its end in the creek!" The men scrambled down from their horses and the wagon.

"Daniel is on his head!" Frank said, nearly in tears. "Now what are we going to do? And where's the lid?"

"Calm down," James said. "Get a hold of yourself. We've got to get Daniel and the coffin out of the water and find the lid. Come on, fellows. Help me!"

Thomas and Billy got in the icy creek with James. Before they could reach it, the coffin shifted and Daniel's body fell forward and into the water. The men almost fell themselves as they worked to get the body picked up. They struggled in the veneer of ice on the edges of the water, their feet sometimes breaking through as they carried the body to the creek bank.

Then they had to get back in the water to get the coffin. Thomas spotted the lid, which had been carried thirty feet down stream by the current. He retrieved it and joined the others on the bank.

"How will we ever tell Hannah that Daniel fell in the creek?" Frank sobbed, his teeth chattering. "She went to all that trouble to get him cleaned up and dressed him up so proper-like."

"We aren't going to tell Hannah, you idiot!" James said. "She has been through enough today. She doesn't need to know the circumstances. All she needs to know is that the coffin slid out of the wagon coming up the hill, and I suspect she's already figured that out."

The men shivered more than ever, now in wet clothes. They quickly put Daniel's body back in the coffin. His clothes were muddy and dripping wet. James reached and wiped the hair out of Daniel's face. "Goodbye again, brother," James said. "Does anybody have any nails on them?" he asked, as he patted his pockets and found none. They all shook their heads.

"These nails are bent all to pieces," James said. "Somebody get me that hammer out from under the wagon seat. We've got to straighten out these nails and use them again."

It took quite a bit of effort and more than a few minutes for James and Thomas to straighten the nails and get the lid re-attached to the coffin.

"Hurry up, boys!" Frank said. "I'm freezing out here!"

"We've all freezing, Frank, no thanks to you," Thomas said. "I still don't see why you didn't see the coffin fall out of the wagon. If you had gotten us stopped when it happened, it wouldn't have been so bad. But no, you had to let us get all the way to the graveyard."

"Stop blaming him," Billy said. "We were all there. Nobody saw it or heard it."

James said nothing.

Frank said nothing.

The men got the coffin back into the wagon and started up the hill to the church. Water was still dripping out of the pine coffin.

****

"Here they come! I'll go get Hannah and the others," John said.

"Hold on there. Considering the way things have gone so far, I think we'd better make sure they have Daniel's body with them before we go making any announcements," Rev. Matthews cautioned.

"Good idea. Let's go," John said and he and Rev. Matthews started walking to meet the wagon party near the grave site.

"Well?" Rev. Matthews asked as he approached the wagon.

Frank jumped in to explain. "Preacher, we found him standing on his head right smack in the middle of Antlers Creek. The lid had popped off the coffin and...."

"Now, Frank," James quickly interrupted, "I don't think the preacher wants to hear all the details. The important thing is we recovered Daniel's body. Come on, boys," he said, motioning to the other pall-bearers. "Let's get the body over there so Rev. Matthews can say some nice things over Daniel and we can get home. It's getting plumb dark!"

"I'll go get Hannah and the other folks from the church," John said, and he hurried back to the sanctuary.

John helped Hannah to her feet and back to the graveside. The gray sky hung heavy with the promise of more snow. The oak trees below the graveyard shuddered in the cold wind and sounded as though they would snap.

The small group of mourners huddled close together for warmth. The day had been an unexpected ordeal for all of them. Rev. Matthews could sense that at this late hour each of them – even Hannah – just wanted to get the service over with so they could go home and try to get warm. He made his remarks as brief as possible for it to still be a respectable service.

"Daniel was a hard worker and good provider," Rev. Matthews said, to which there was a less than enthusiastic "Amen" from one of the mourners.

"He was a good friend and neighbor," Rev. Matthews continued. After a long pause, someone in the back finally said, "Amen."

"He will be missed," Rev. Matthews added. "Unless someone has something they would like to say, I'm going to have the closing prayer now so we can all head home to try to get warm." There were nods of encouragement from several mourners, so the pastor began to pray.

Hannah's shoulders sagged as Rev. Matthews prayed, but then she took a deep breath and straightened her tired back. She suddenly felt a great relief, as if a heavy burden had been lifted from her. When the service ended, Rev. Matthews and the mourners spoke to Hannah one-by-one and offered any support of assistance they could. James stepped forward to comfort her.

"I'm sorry... for everything," James said to Hannah as he took her hands and held them in his. "I'm sorry about Daniel. You did all you could for him. I'm sorry about the delay in the service. I would offer to take you home, but I need to get home and get out of these wet clothes."

"That's all right. John will take me home. Thank you for all you've done. I will see you soon?" Hannah asked as she hugged him.

"Yes, I'll come by in the morning to build up your fire and see about the animals," James said.

With Daniel finally out of the way, I can have a future with James! Hannah thought. She had to steel herself lest someone noticed her smiling. She slowly felt the small, envelope which was still in her skirt pocket. *Yes, that was the best purchase I ever made!*

Author's Note: I wrote the original version of "Slip Sliding Away" in 2003 while a member of Queens Writers Group in Charlotte, North Carolina. All members of the group had completed Judith Simpson's "Foundations in Fiction" writing course in the continuing education department at Queens University of Charlotte. "Slip Sliding Away" was chosen as the lead story in *Tales for a Long Winter's Night*, a collection of winter-themed short stories written by members of Queens Writers Group.

Janet has rewritten and edited the story many times between 2003 and 2023. In 2023, she self-published "Slip Sliding Away" as a standalone southern historical short story.

A Plott Hound Called Buddy

Lois lived alone in the Victorian-era farmhouse in which she was born. Her closest neighbor was more than a mile away. She loved the North Carolina mountains where she had lived her entire life.

A retired teacher, she had tried to instill a pride in place in her students. She taught all eleven grades in a one-room schoolhouse that her father helped build. She led a quiet, solitary life now for the most part, but she could not imagine living anywhere else.

Lois opened her back door just after daylight one April morning and was surprised to find a dog lying on the stoop.

"Top o' the morning to you," Lois said. "What's your name, young fella?"

The yellow brindle dog whined and looked up at Lois with its big brown eyes.

"Are you one of those Plott hounds?" Lois asked. "You look well-fed and healthy. I believe somebody's taken good care of you in spite of The Depression."

Lois bent over to get a better look. "On closer inspection, though, I see you've had your share of tangles with other animals. If I didn't know better, I'd say you've been slapped by a bear. I'll need to put some salve on that. I don't know much about hound dogs, but don't they call it 'pulled hair' when a hound bites a bear? Is that what happened, Buddy? I don't know your name, but you look like a 'Buddy' to me. Did you get in a fight with a bear?"

The dog whined and beat his tail on the wood floor of the stoop at the top of three wood plank steps that led to the back door of Lois' old farmhouse.

"Now is that a fact?" Lois asked. "You act like you understand everything I'm saying to you. I'd hate to see the bear!" Lois laughed. "I sure wish you could talk. I'll bet you would have some tales to tell."

Lois looked the dog over without touching him, to see if he had any other wounds. "You look okay otherwise. You can stay here until I figure out who you belong to. My house is a magnet for strays. There seems to be a secret communications system out there among lost and abandoned dogs – sort of like the Underground Railroad."

The dog appeared to hang on her every word.

"Are you hungry, Buddy?" Lois asked. Buddy's tail beat a quick, steady rhythm on the floor.

"That's a 'yes,' if I ever did hear one. Come on in the house." Lois held the door open and snapped her fingers. "It's cold out here and I'm hungry, too."

The dog struggled a little to stand up and get his feet firmly planted under him.

"I see you're stiff like I am of a mornin'. How old are you? I'm 74."

"Buddy" hesitated but then went inside and waited in the back porch until Lois led the way into the kitchen. "Lie down over there by the wood stove," Lois said. "I hope you like cornmeal mush and scrambled eggs. That's what we're having for breakfast. Okay?"

Buddy limped over by the stove and seemed happy to wait for whatever food Lois had to offer.

"I don't know how long you're planning to stay, but we need to get something straight from the start. This ain't no diner. I eat three meals a day, so that's all you get. Whatever I'm eating, you're eating. Any questions?"

Lois looked over to discover that Buddy was sound asleep, his chin resting on the linoleum floor.

"Did you know there's a depression going on?" Lois asked Buddy while she scrambled two extra eggs for him, although he had started snoring.. "They call it The Great Depression, but I don't know what's so great about it. I can't tell much difference. I've always known hard times. My husband died early in the influenza epidemic and then my son, Henry, died in the war. They called it "The Great War," too. Seems to me like calling all these things great doesn't help anybody. They say it was the war to end all wars, but I don't put any stock in that. Do you, Buddy?"

Lois turned to look at the sleeping dog. "Well, I'll be. I might as well be talking to myself. Bless your heart. You must be plumb worn out."

Lois went to the back porch and retrieved two dog bowls from the top shelf. Tears stung her eyes as her mind flashed back to Shad, the beautiful and gentle German Shepherd she used to have. She filled one dish with water and spooned mush and scrambled eggs into the other one. She tested the temperature of the food with her finger and deemed it to be cool enough not to burn Buddy's tongue. He was sleeping so soundly that she had trouble waking him up to eat. Once awake, though, he scarfed down the food like he had not eaten in days. "These bowls belonged to Shad. You would have liked him."

Lois sat down to eat her breakfast. "I just couldn't part with his bowls or his leather collar. It hangs on a nail in the back porch. That's how much I loved that dog. Does someone love you like that, Buddy?"

No sooner had he finished eating than he started noisily lapping up the water. He quickly emptied the water dish and looked at Lois as if to say, "More!"

"Let me finish my breakfast."

Buddy changed his mind after a couple of minutes and went to the back door. When Lois had swallowed her last bite of food and last swig of coffee, she got up and found the dog sitting quietly with his nose pointing to the door knob.

"Okay," Lois said. "Go on out and do what you need to do, but then stay in the yard. Someone's bound to come looking for you sooner or later."

She went back to the kitchen and washed the breakfast dishes, including Buddy's two bowls. Then she went to the back door and pulled back the curtains to look out the window that filled the upper half of the door. Buddy lay in the sun in the backyard, just a few feet from the bottom of the steps.

"He thinks he's found himself a home," Lois said out loud, "but the last thing I need is a hound dog."

Several days went by. No one inquired about a missing dog. Lois wished she had a telephone or a way to go into town so she could tell the sheriff about Buddy. She was sure the dog belonged to somebody.

That night she carried her oil lamp to the back door and peered out the window. Buddy appeared to be sound asleep on the stoop, so Lois went to bed. At two o'clock, Lois shot straight up. Buddy's high-pitched, choppy voice sent chills down her spine. It was the first time she had heard him bark.

Lois reached for her robe and slid her feet into her bedroom slippers as she put the robe on. She grabbed her rifle from under the bed. When she looked out the back door window she saw Buddy in the moonlight at the hen house door. His tail was raised high and he appeared to be ready and able to take on whomever or whatever had intruded his territory. The chickens were in an uproar.

By the time Lois got to the hen house, Buddy was trying to get the door open. "Good boy," she said. "Whatever it is, I don't believe it has a chance against the two of us."

As soon as she opened the hen house door, a red fox darted out with one of her prize hens in its mouth. Buddy lit in after the fox with Lois yelling for him to stop. Much to her surprise, he stopped fairly soon and started back toward the scene of the crime.

Lois was muttering under her breath and counting dead chickens when Buddy returned and nuzzled her hand. "Five dead, plus the one the fox took with him." Lois shook her head and started mentally calculating how many eggs that meant she would be short the next week when Mr. Leatherwood would stop by to buy eggs to sell at his mercantile in Asheville. The eggs brought in precious little money for Lois, but every penny was already anticipated and allocated before she made it.

"Looks like we'll have to cut back on scrambled eggs, Buddy. Maybe you and I can split one every once in a while for a treat. It's a good thing we both like mush for breakfast and beans for lunch and supper. You stand guard while I try to get the remaining chickens to simmer down."

Lois got a tow sack out of the barn and went back to gather up the chicken carcasses. She knew each chicken individually and it broke her heart in more ways than just financially to see the carnage left behind by that fox. She would burn the carcasses at first light.

Ordinarily, Lois would have spent the rest of the night on the back stoop, watching the chicken coop; however, on this night she was confident that Buddy had the situation under control.

"Goodnight, Buddy," she said. "I wish I could reward you with some eggs or chicken, but I don't want you to dare get the taste of raw chicken. You keep watch until daylight and then I'll come out and finish taking care of the mess." She stooped down to pat the dog on his head. "Good dog. You earned your keep tonight. Maybe I need a dog after all. What do you think?"

Buddy cocked his head and looked up at Lois. He wagged his tail, and Lois knew that meant that he thought she not only needed a dog but that she needed him. By the time Lois reached the back door, Buddy had laid claim to the hen house and was keeping watch.

No sooner than Lois had gotten back in bed, she realized that she had forgotten to secure the hen house door. She got up and went back outside. Buddy watched her go to the barn and return with a log. She propped the log up against the hen house door. "No fox will be able to move this," she said. She gave Buddy a pat on the head and wished him a quiet rest of the night.

Even though Lois was sure Buddy would alert her if the fox set foot on her farm, she laid awake the rest of the night. The next day was tiring for Lois and Buddy after the trauma of the night and their lack of sleep. Burning the chicken carcasses was unpleasant in more ways than one. She gagged and cried even after the task was done.

The next day and night were uneventful. No one came by to inquire about a missing dog, and Buddy seemed happy to stay. Lois began to relax a little and fall back into a normal routine of sleeping through the night.

But the following night, she was awakened once again by Buddy's high-pitched voice. He didn't howl like other hound dogs she had known of. She wondered what kind of hound he was, but she didn't have time to think long. She put on her robe and slippers, grabbed her rifle, and headed to the back door and the direction of the racket.

Lois just could see Buddy in the edge of the woods, his tail up and still. "What is it? Have you treed a raccoon or 'possum?"

She slowly walked to the hen house door where she stopped in her tracks and listened. Everything seemed to be all right in there.

Suddenly, she heard the unmistakable growl of a black bear. It was close by in the woods, but she could not see it in the dark. She knew she was in danger because the bear had, no doubt, been attracted by the smell of blood and raw chicken even though she had done her best to clean up the mess. And here she stood at the hen house door.

Not knowing anything about Plott Hounds, Lois had no idea that black bears were sheer fun for Buddy. She trembled for a moment as the breeze kicked up and she contemplated what to do. The bear was somewhere downwind of her.

Lois was a good shot with a rifle in the daylight, but she had never tried to shoot a black bear at night. She thought about just shooting into the sky, but that might incite the bear to charge. Now she could hear it breathing. It sounded like it was moving through the trees to the side of the hen house.

Lois knew it was never a good idea to run from a bear, but she looked at the back of the house anyway and wondered if she could outrun this one. Her heart pounded in her chest and ears, making it difficult to follow the sounds of the bear.

"You distract him, Buddy," she said. "I've got to try to get back to the house."

No sooner had Lois lit out toward the house than Buddy lit in after the bear. Lois cleared the back steps and slammed the door safely behind her. She watched the bear lumber toward the hen house door with Buddy on its heels. She watched in amazement as the 400-pound bear turned around, stood up on its hind legs, and challenged Buddy.

"Buddy, no!" Lois screamed. She stepped out on the back stoop and aimed her rifle at the bear. She could not get a clear shot off. Buddy showed no fear as he lunged at the bear's face. The bear growled and swatted at the 60-pound hound. Lois fired a shot into the air, to no avail. Neither bear nor hound paid any attention to the blast which echoed off the woods.

Lois had never witnessed such a struggle in her life and she was shocked at the fearlessness and stamina Buddy showed in the face of what looked to her like sure death for the dog. She fired her rifle into the air once again, but the fight continued with neither animal appearing to take an advantage.

Just then, the bear swatted at Buddy, knocking the dog into the hen house wall and then to the ground. With that, the bear dropped down on all fours and shook its head from side-to-side. Buddy lay still on the ground.

"Come on, Buddy!" Lois yelled. "Get up! Get up, Buddy!"

Suddenly, Buddy leapt to his feet and flew into the bear with all his power and strength. The hound drew back and Lois saw that he had a mouth full of bear fur. The bear turned and ran with Buddy on his heels.

Lois continued to hear Buddy's high-pitched voice getting farther and farther away as he chased the bear deep into the woods. She stood on the back stoop, listening for Buddy for 20 minutes.

When she could no longer hear the dog, she went inside the house, slid the rifle under her bed, and sat down at the kitchen table to collect her thoughts. She was tempted to take a headache powder to settle her raw nerves, but thought better of it. If anything else happened that night, she would need her wits about her.

Unable to sleep, Lois sat up all night hoping to hear Buddy at the back door. It was not yet daylight when she heard a scratch at the door.

"Please let it be Buddy," she prayed as she hurried to the door. She pulled the curtains back and peered out the door window. "Buddy!"

When she opened the door, the exhausted and bloody Plott Hound immediately lay down at her feet on the stoop. "I'm so glad to see you, Buddy," she said. "I was worried sick all night. Is that your blood or the bear's?"

Buddy was too tired to lift his head. "I think most of it is from the bear," Lois said. "You rest while I get a rag and some water to clean you up, and then I'll fix us some breakfast. You more than earned your keep last night. I think I'll keep you if that's all right with you and your owner doesn't show up looking for you."

When she came out to wash the blood off Buddy, he was sound asleep. Lois kneeled beside him and gently wiped dried blood out of his short coat. It was then that she discovered that one of his eyes was swollen shut. She went inside and retrieved the tin of salve. Buddy winced when she applied the ointment to his eye but seemed to know she was trying to help him.

Lois poured out the dirty water and went inside to cook breakfast, Buddy on her heels. She cooked the only egg she had and a big pot of cornmeal mush. When the food was ready, she put all the scrambled egg in Buddy's bowl. She put the mush on a couple of plates to cool while she fed him the egg. He inhaled it while Lois refilled his water dish. As soon as she brought his mush out and scraped it into his food dish, he gobbled it up like he had never had anything to eat.

"That's enough for now," Lois said. "It's my turn."

Just then, a rare pair of headlights shown up her driveway. Lois craned her neck and squinted in the twilight to see that it was a stranger – a man in bib overalls.

"Sampson!" the man exclaimed as he jumped out of his Model-T Ford.

"Buddy" woke up at the sound of his real name and the voice of his master and ran to the door.

Lois opened the door and Buddy, a.k.a., Sampson, bounded down the steps. He and the man had a joyful reunion.

"Excuse my manners, ma'am," the man said. "Sampson's my prize Plott hound. I've been all over the county looking for him. I hope he's not put you out too much."

"On the contrary," Lois said. "He saved my life last night when a black bear came up in the yard. He chased that bear all night. That's how his eye got messed up. I put some salve on it."

"Much obliged," the man said. "Here's a dollar for your trouble. It's all I have."

"No," Lois said. "I won't take your money. I was glad to keep him. He lived up to his name last night when he took on that bear. I've been calling him 'Buddy,' but 'Sampson' seems more appropriate."

The man nodded his thanks and said, "Come on, Sampson. Let's go home."

Lois wiped a tear from her cheek and watched until the Model-T disappeared down the road. "It worked out for the best," Lois said to herself. "Buddy – I mean Sampson -- was here when I needed him, but he had to go home. I sure will miss him! Maybe I need to get a dog."

Author's Note:

I have loved dogs all my life, but I've never had a hound dog. The Plott Hound was named the official State Dog of North Carolina in 1989. This breed of dog was developed by Henry Plott, the son of German immigrant Johannes Plott in the 1700s in North Carolina. The dog was bred to hunt bears. Registered with the United Kennel Club in 1946, the Plott Hound was recognized by the American Kennel Club in 2006 and first exhibited at the Westminster Show in 2008.

Secrets of a Foster Child

December 1948

The Lockharts' biological daughter, Kathy, and I shared a bedroom. We had twin beds with matching bed linens. The pink curtains even matched the bedspreads. Everything in the room was color-coordinated. I'd never seen anything like it.

For a 12-year-old, Kathy was a master of the poker face. I could never tell what she was thinking, but I could read Mr. and Mrs. Lockhart and most other adults like a book.

I had become good at reading adults and knowing when it was time to move on. At the age of 14, I had had plenty of practice.

Kathy and I were in her bedroom — it didn't feel like my room yet. I was reading *Romeo and Juliet* for tomorrow's test, but I was bored. The language was hard to understand. "Wherefore art thou, Romeo?" I mean, who talks like that? It didn't matter. None of it mattered. Kathy was humming "Buttons and Bows." I put my book down on the bed. Hoping for a bit of fun with Kathy, I started singing the words as Kathy hummed. She joined me and we pretended we were Dinah Shore. A love of music was the only thing we had in common.

"Lorraine, come here, please," Mrs. Lockhart said from the foot of the stairs.

We stopped singing. "Coming," I answered. I wondered if I was about to be punished for singing when I was supposed to be studying. I hurried downstairs.

"Yes, ma'am?" I said when I found Mrs. Lockhart sitting at the small dining table in the breakfast nook. I had never lived in a house with so many rooms and nooks and crannies before.

"Have a seat. I thought you might like a cup of hot chocolate."

"Thank you. It smells good!" I slid onto the bench across the table from her. Her face was tense. The vertical lines between her eyes reached farther up into her forehead than usual. I braced myself for bad news.

"Mr. Lockhart and I are afraid that, due to our lack of foster care experience, we've done you a disservice."

I stared into the swirl of whipped cream that was rapidly melting into my hot chocolate. I knew her pause was my cue to respond. Several responses went through my head, but the permanent chip on my shoulder prevented me from saying a word.

"Are you aware that you are our first foster child?" Mrs. Lockhart asked.

"Yes." I gave her the best steely stare I could muster.

Mrs. Lockhart did not hide her surprise over my affirmative answer. Her hand trembled as she pushed her hair behind her ear.

I did not blink. I had long ago tired of trying to make foster parents feel good or make these "Don't take this personally, but you've got to go" speeches easy for the adults.

"I don't recall telling you," she said. Another long pause followed during which I said nothing. "Mindy, why do you make everything so difficult? How did you know?"

"I figured it out the first day. I knew right off the bat that I had a lot more experience with foster care than y'all did."

"It was that obvious?"

I rolled my eyes. "This is my sixth foster home. I can spot a rookie a mile away."

"We've tried to treat you like you're our own daughter. Tell me where you think we've gotten it wrong."

"It's not so much you as it is me." I put on my best adult voice and tried to speak matter-of-factly. "I can't let my guard down. Nothing in my life has ever been permanent. I can't let myself think any relationships are going to last. Kathy said she had always wanted a sister but after she got one – me – she decided it wasn't all it was cracked up to be. I knew then that my time here was limited." As soon as those words came out of my mouth, I wished I could take them back.

"I'm sorry she said that."

"It's okay. She didn't mean it. After being moved from one family to another, I learned not to get close. It's too painful when it's time to leave. I call it 'putting my tough on.' I'm able to call it up and put it on in a split second." Surprised at myself for giving more than a one-word answer – and spilling my guts about being able to "put my tough on," I didn't know what else to say. I lifted the Christmas mug to my lips and noisily sipped at the delicious steaming chocolate.

"Miss Hurley senses you aren't happy here. She called yesterday and suggested that you spend the holidays with another family. How does that sound to you?" Her voice quivered.

Miss Hurley was my caseworker. We discussed on more than one occasion the reasons adolescents and teenagers were more difficult to place in foster homes than cute little children with blue eyes and blond curls. She had always been honest with me. She told me that I could forget about being adopted if I was not by the time I turned twelve.

I shrugged and sat quietly for several minutes. "Whatever," I said. I added a predictable eyeroll. "Whatever you and Miss Hurley think." Another move. My eyes stung with tears. I dropped my head so Mrs. Lockhart would not see. I hated it when I cried.

"I want to know what you think. You're old enough to have a say in this. Mr. Lockhart and I are willing to try to make this work, if you want to give us another chance. We want to do whatever is best for you. We'd love for you to be with us for Christmas, but if you'd prefer to go to another family for Christmas break we won't be upset with you. Your happiness and safety are our main concern."

I was not used to being asked my opinion about anything. This unexpected turn of events made me uncomfortable. Did this mean the Lockharts would seek my opinion on other things if I stayed? The part of me that was straining to be an adult liked those prospects, but the part of me that was still a child was unnerved at the prospect of being asked what I thought or wanted. No one had ever cared or asked if I had an opinion. All decisions were made for me.

If I had a dollar for every time a case worker or a foster parent had said, "This is for your own good," in the last nine years, I would have enough money to buy one of those new Buick Super Convertibles complete with white wall tires and rear wheel fenders!

"This is for your own good." It was the first time that I heard those words that hurt the most. When my biological father said them the last time we talked, which was when I was five years old, it stung my heart and caused a tightening in my throat as if a noose were around my neck.

"We want to give you a home and family as long as you want to stay here," Mrs. Lockhart said. "You're a private person and we have hesitated to pry. Perhaps we would understand you better if we knew more about you."

My heart raced, and I wanted to run.

"I wouldn't know where to start. What do you want to know?"

"Anything you feel comfortable talking about. You can tell us in confidence."

I grew more nervous. No one had ever asked me to tell my life story before. I had yearned for another human being to be that interested in me, but the memory of overhearing some of my former foster parents' telephone conversations with friends made me doubt the "in confidence" aspect.

"You can trust me," Mrs. Lockhart said. It was as if she read my thoughts, and I desperately wanted to trust her. I had no reason to doubt her words. Maybe I'd been wrong to lump her in the same basket with one or two of those other women who had passed in and out of my life. Most of my foster parents meant well.

"It all started with the fire." As soon as I said the words, I wished I could retrieve them. I chewed on my lower lip and looked around the room.

"Tell me about the fire." Mrs. Lockhart sounded sincere and looked me in the eye.

I took a deep breath, put my tough on, and dived in. "My twin sister and I were playing with our dolls in our room. Her name was Linda. I smelled smoke and ran to look for Mama. She had fallen asleep again with a cigarette in her hand. The bed was on fire around her. I tried to wake her up, but she wouldn't wake up." I stopped to catch my breath.

"Take your time," Mrs. Lockhart said.

I took another swig of my hot chocolate. "My daddy said later that she wasn't sleeping. He said she was drunk. I was too young to understand, after all, I was just five years old. But getting back to the fire, it was getting really hot. The curtains were burning and melting. The smoke burned my eyes and I started choking. I ran to get Linda to help me wake up Mama, but Linda was crying and had locked herself in the bathroom. I couldn't get her to come out."

My "tough" started failing me and I felt tears running down my cheeks. Mrs. Lockhart got up, gave me a tissue, and put her arm around my shoulders. She placed a gentle kiss on the top of my head. After another deep breath, I continued.

"I couldn't get Linda to come out, and I couldn't wake up Mama. Linda said she was too scared to come out. The smoke was getting thicker. My eyes were burning. I ran back to try again to wake up Mama, but she didn't move and didn't say anything. I ran down the hall and begged Linda to come with me, but she refused. The hall ceiling was on fire by then and chunks of it were dropping all around me."

"How awful for you," Mrs. Lockhart said, barely above a whisper. She held me closer to her and it felt right. It felt comfortable, like a real mother would draw her child close to her side.

"I ran outside just as the roof collapsed. I tried to save them! I tried! I really tried!"

"If you had stayed in there a few more seconds, you might have died in that fire," Mrs. Lockhart said. "You can't blame yourself for their deaths. You were just five years old."

I knew she was trying to console me, but I do not think I will ever forgive myself for letting Mama and Melly die in that fire. There must have been something I could have done.

"After I got outside, I screamed and cried. There was nothing else I could do. We lived out in the country. It was too far for me to run to a neighbor's house. I didn't know what to do. Sometime later – I don't know how long – a car went by, stopped, backed up, and drove into our driveway. The driver jumped out of the car. He asked if anyone was still in the house. Between coughs, I told him where Mama and Linda were. He went all around the house, but he couldn't get in. The fire was too hot. He told me to stay back from the fire but out of the street. I was still coughing, and every time I coughed, smoke came out of my mouth. The man said he'd go to the next house to call the volunteer fire department, but it was of no use. He came back after what seemed like an hour and said the fire truck was on its way. He held my hand as we watched the entire house engulf in flames. A fire truck and an ambulance came. They put me in the ambulance and took me to the hospital. I spent a couple of nights there. They couldn't find my father."

I stopped to catch my breath. I could not believe how easily and fast the facts of that horrible day were spilling out of my mouth. It was like a sudden crack in a dam that had been straining to hold back flood waters for nine years.

"Where was your father?" Mrs. Lockhart asked.

"He was a long-distance truck driver. He was gone for weeks at a time, and I didn't know where he was or how to call him. The police or the nurse at the hospital called the Welfare Department. That was the beginning of my life as a foster child."

"When did your father come home?"

"I don't know. I never saw him again."

"Never?"

"Never. It was about six months after the fire that he contacted the Welfare Department and found out where I was. He called me and said he couldn't take care of me on the road and staying in foster care was 'for my own good.'" I winced as I said the words. I swallowed hard against the taste of bile in my throat before I could continue. "He said he loved me and that was the end of the conversation. He never called me again. Of course, I kept moving around. He might have tried but couldn't find me."

"Surely the Welfare Department could have – I mean, that's true," Mrs. Lockhart said. "I'm sure he has tried and he must have loved you very much to give you up. It would have been impossible for you to grow up on the road. School would have been a real problem. I'm sure he thought he was doing the best thing for you under the circumstances. Do you have grandparents or aunts and uncles?"

"I don't think so."

"You have had more sorrow and heartbreak than most people have in a lifetime," Mrs. Lockhart said. "I am so sorry." She hugged me like she really meant it.

"You don't know the half of it," I said. "Some of my foster families have been less than stellar."

Mrs. Lockhart looked surprised.

"Stellar is my new word and I've been looking for the perfect time to casually work it into a sentence. Did I use it correctly?"

"Yes," Mrs. Lockhart said. "I'm here to listen if you ever want to talk about any of your foster experiences. I don't mean like gossiping, of course, but sometimes it helps a person heal to talk about the bad times in their lives."

"Okay."

"What do you want me to tell Miss Hurley?"

"Tell her I'd like to stay here, if it's all right with you and Mr. Lockhart – and Kathy."

Mrs. Lockhart smiled. "Of course, it's all right! It's more than 'all right;' it's great!" She hugged me again, and that time I hugged back. A little part of me felt like I was at home, but the larger part of me – the part that had been hurt so many times – told me not to get used to the idea.

Just as I reached the stairs, Mrs. Lockhart called my name.

"Yes?"

"When you call us 'Mr. and Mrs. Lockhart' it sounds too stiff and formal. You may call us 'Mom' and 'Dad,' if you wish. Or you may call us by our given names, Laura and David. Whatever you feel comfortable with will be all right with us."

"I'll need to think about that for a while."

When I went back upstairs to the bedroom, Kathy was anxiously waiting for me. I closed the door and sat down on my bed to face her.

"Well?" she asked.

"Well what?"

"What was that all about? You aren't leaving, are you?"

"No. We had a nice conversation. I feel more comfortable with your mother now."

"To tell you the truth, I thought you were leaving and I thought I'd be glad. I was lonesome while you were talking to Mom just now, and I realized I would miss you if you had to go to another foster home."

"I would miss you, too," I said.

"I feel closer to you than I have since you moved in."

"Let's try to finish our homework before dinner," I said. "I have a test tomorrow on *Romeo and Juliet* and I haven't finished reading it yet." I snuggled up in my bed, which suddenly felt right to me, and finished reading the play.

Mr. Lockhart came in from his job at the bank, and I could hear him and Mrs. Lockhart talking. I could not understand a word they said, but I assumed that Mrs. Lockhart was telling him about our conversation and that I was not moving on after all.

Yes, I am still referring to them as Mr. and Mrs. Lockhart. I am going to have to ease into calling them Mom and Dad. For one thing, it might make Kathy feel weird.

"Dinner's ready!" Mrs. Lockhart called from the landing on the stairs.

Kathy and I raced to see who could get to the bathroom to wash hands first. We were still laughing when we got to the dining room. Mr. Lockhart looked especially serious. Mrs. Lockhart had been crying.

We all sat down at our usual places at the table. I thought about how nice it would be to know that was my chair at hundreds of meals in the future. My mind was still wondering about that and imagining sitting down there for family dinners for months or even years down the road when Mrs. Lockhart announced that she thought it would be nice for us to hold hands around the table while Mr. Lockhart said grace. I liked that. I thought how I could get used to this family and I was so thankful they were giving me a second chance.

Mr. Lockhart gave thanks for the food we were about to eat; for giving Mrs. Lockhart the gift of preparing it; for good health, safety, and security; and for giving him a job that provided enough income to provide the necessities of life for "the four of us." I especially liked that last part.

Mrs. Lockhart was a great cook, and Mr. Lockhart's income made it possible for us to eat well. Many nights there were cuts of meat for dinner that I couldn't identify. I wondered if I would ever be able to cook like Mrs. Lockhart. I'd have to learn the different cuts of meats first, though, and have a high-paying job. If I had a husband with a high-paying job, that would be okay, too, but I decided the day our house burned down and my daddy didn't have the decency to even come home and give me a hug – much less two dimes to rub together – that when I grew up I would never be dependent on a man for money, food, clothes, transportation, or a roof over my head. Women didn't have many options for jobs, especially since the war ended and the men came home, but I was determined to support myself when I grew up.

As we took our last bites of dinner, Mr. Lockhart said he had something to tell us. His tone and facial expression made a knot the size of a grapefruit form in my stomach. "I got some news today," he said. "On one hand, it was good news, but in another way it was bad news."

My stomach clinched along with my teeth. I braced myself for the bad part.

"What is it, Daddy?" Kathy asked.

"I was promoted to senior vice president."

"That's great! So what's the bad part?" Kathy asked.

"The promotion means we'll have to move to New York City, and the bad part is that Lorraine won't be able to go with us. I'm truly sorry, Lorraine."

I knew he said there was bad news, but somehow I did not see that coming. I did not have time to "put my tough on." My head was spinning. Mr. Lockhart was still talking, but I did not hear a word he said. I don't know how long I sat there in shock before I felt Mrs. Lockhart's arms wrap around me from behind. She kissed the top of my head and then rested her head there. I soon felt her tears in my hair.

"When?" I whispered when I got able to speak.

"Over the Christmas holidays," Mrs. Lockhart said.

"But that's just a couple of weeks away," Kathy said. "This isn't fair! I was just starting to like Lorraine!" With that, Kathy stomped to our room and slammed the door.

I was numb. Mr. and Mrs. Lockhart tried to make me feel better, but things looked very bleak from where I sat. They now sat on either side of me.

"I'll miss you," I said through my tears. I looked at Mrs. Lockhart. "Our talk this afternoon was just the best. It made me feel like I belonged here. I should have known it was too good to be true."

Mr. and Mrs. Lockhart kept apologizing to me for smashing my dreams, and I soon found myself comforting them. Relationships in my life seem to always get turned upside down.

Kathy and I went through the motions of going to school for the two weeks remaining before the Christmas break. Mrs. Lockhart spent most of her time packing. By the time I lived with that activity and stress for a few days, I decided that owning a lot of things maybe was not such a great thing after all. Mrs. Lockhart seemed overwhelmed with the task of packing everything that she, Kathy, and Mr. Lockhart owned. I could not imagine ever owning that much stuff.

Friday of the second week came before I was ready for it. I didn't know where I would be living and going to school in January, so I didn't know whether to tell my classmates goodbye or not. Everyone else at school could not wait for the holidays, but I dreaded them more than any of my life – and that is saying a lot because I have had some pretty bleak Christmases.

The first Christmas after Mama and Linda died was the worst. Daddy did not come or call or even send a card. The one when all the biological children in the foster home got presents but I got none was another one I would like to forget. The memory of all my Christmases came flooding back to me as I rode home on the school bus that afternoon. The other students laughed and talked all around me, but I was lost in my own world – a world that was crashing in on me, one more time.

Kathy and I got off the bus and headed straight to the kitchen to look for snacks. We both chose apple juice and peanut butter on saltine crackers. But before we sat down, Mrs. Lockhart told Kathy she could eat in our bedroom. She said she needed to talk to me. Suddenly, I was not hungry. Kathy and I looked at each other. Kathy shrugged and shook her head, which told me that she didn't know what this was about. I shrugged back and slid into my usual place on the breakfast nook bench.

Mrs. Lockhart sat down beside me and immediately concentrated on making sharp, crisp pleats in a paper napkin. You would have thought she was being judged on precision. She had trouble looking me in the eye.

"Are you going to tell me when I have to leave?" I asked.

Mrs. Lockhart seemed unable to speak. Her lips trembled and she continued to stare at the pleated napkin.

"I'll take that as a 'yes,'" I said. "Do you know if I'll have to change schools?"

"No, I don't."

"That's the worst part, usually."

"What's the worst part when you don't have to change schools?" she asked.

"Sometimes, there's abuse. That's always in the back of my mind when I have to move in with a new family. I've learned not to trust people until they earn my trust."

Mrs. Lockhart's mouth dropped open. Her eyes filled with tears. The palm of her hand pressed against her chest. "Please tell me you aren't serious about the abuse."

I aim to please, so I said, "No, I was kidding."

"Good," she said. "Miss Hurley called this morning. She'll be here at nine o'clock in the morning to take you to meet your new foster parents. She said they're very nice people."

"I'm sure they are," I said for her benefit, and I wanted to believe it myself. "If that's all you had to tell me, I guess I'll go pack my things although that won't take more than five minutes."

"That's all. I'll save your apple juice," she said. "Maybe you'll want it later. I washed your clothes today, I didn't want you going to your next home with a bunch of dirty clothes. I want you to make a good first impression, and I don't want your new foster mother thinking I'm a slob." She attempted to laugh but broke down in tears instead.

"Thank you. I'll do my best." I wanted to laugh to lighten up the moment, but I couldn't pull it off.

I started down the hall toward the stairs but stopped and looked back at Mrs. Lockhart. Tears streamed down her cheeks. Part of me wanted to run and hug her, but the rest of me thought she should be comforting me.

I went to Kathy's bedroom. It was no longer half mine. I pulled the old wrinkled brown paper grocery bag out of my drawer in the chest-of-drawers Kathy and I shared. The bag was my suitcase. It seemed appropriate that I could fit all my worldly possessions into a paper bag because I had always been a throwaway kid. That is how foster children sometimes feel. It is not our fault, and it's not necessarily the fault of the foster parents. It's just the way it is, and I doubt there is any way around it.

"Are you moving out tonight?" Kathy asked.

"No, in the morning. Nine o'clock."

"Where are you going?"

"I don't know. Miss Hurley didn't tell your mother. She just said they're nice people."

"I'll miss you," Kathy said. "I was just getting used to having a sister."

"Yeah, me, too."

"Mom said we wasted too much time being standoffish."

"It's hard for me to get close to people because I know everything is temporary."

"After being an only child all my life, I didn't know how to be a sister to you. I'll try to be a better sister if we get another foster child after we move to New York."

"Me, too. I'll try not to be so defensive at my next home."

"I guess we've both learned something through all this," Kathy said.

"Yeah, I guess we have. Too bad we didn't learn it until our last couple of weeks together."

"Will you write me a letter after you move? You know our address for a few more days, but I won't know yours."

"Yeah, I'll write you, but you'd better write me back."

"I will," Kathy said. "I promise."

"Girls," Mrs. Lockhart said, and then she tapped on the door. "I've set up the card table so the four of us can play Sorry. Come to the living room when you're ready."

I turned to Kathy and whispered, "I don't know how to play Sorry."

"Don't worry," she said. "It's easy and a lot of fun. We used to play it all the time."

Kathy and I hurried to the den. I had never played a board game before.

"I found the game in a closet today while I was packing," Mrs. Lockhart said. "I hadn't thought about Sorry in a long time. Lorraine, which color do you want to be?"

I looked at the choices and picked red, my favorite color.

Kathy explained the rules to me. In a few minutes we were laughing and having a good time.

"Let's play it again!" I said, when we finished the first game. "That was fun, and I didn't even win."

Everyone agreed to play the game a second time. Things were going fine until I realized that no one was using their Sorry cards to send my game pieces back to "Start."

"Okay, y'all," I said. "That's not fair. If you love me, you'll send me back to 'Start' sometimes."

They all looked a little sheepish, and then promised to pick on me as much as they'd been picking on each other. The game was hilarious. I don't know when I've ever laughed so much. It gave me a good memory from my last night in the Lockharts' home. It was ironic that now that I was leaving, we were finally comfortable with each other. We finally felt like a real family.

"Tomorrow is a big day for all of us," Mrs. Lockhart said when we finished the second game. "I think we need to get a good night's sleep."

We said our goodnights and went to bed. I couldn't sleep for wondering what my next family would be like and where I would go to school in January. I thought daylight would never come but, when it arrived, I wished I could turn back the clock. As soon as the wonderful smell of bacon and eggs wafted under the bedroom door, though, I was eager for Mrs. Lockhart to call us to breakfast.

Kathy and I raced to the breakfast table. It was odd, though. The very food that had made my mouth water a few minutes earlier held no appeal when I sat down to eat.

"Try to eat your grits and some egg," Mrs. Lockhart said. The words of encouragement seemed to be directed at me. "They'll stick to your ribs and get you through the morning."

I wanted to tell her I would eat, but there was a lump in my throat. I tried to clear my throat.

"Or at least a piece of toast or some cereal," she continued. "Whatever you want."

"The eggs and grits are fine," I said. "Will I be at the new family's house for lunch?"

"I don't know," Mrs. Lockhart said. "I suppose so, but Miss Hurley didn't say."

"Seems like there was a lot Miss Hurley didn't say," Kathy said. She went to the bedroom in tears.

Mr. Lockhart went outside to get the morning newspaper. I helped Mrs. Lockhart clear the table. Our eyes met and she reached with her free hand and gently but firmly grasped my forearm.

"Were you serious about the abuse at some of the foster homes you've been in?" she asked.

"Yes."

"I thought so, but I didn't want to hear it. It has bothered me for two weeks. What kind of abuse?"

"Every kind you can think of, but that was just at one home. I was treated all right everywhere else. A couple of families saw me as a way to get a check from the county every month, but they were struggling. I couldn't really blame them for trying to make some extra money by taking me in. They weren't abusive. A couple of foster parents decided that foster care wasn't what they wanted to do after all. One couple was out to change the world, one foster child at a time. I was their first and last project."

"Did the abuse take place at the home where you were prior to coming here?" Mrs. Lockhart asked.

"No, it was a couple of homes ago."

"I'm sorry we didn't know. Did you tell Miss Hurley?"

"Yes. She got me out of there that day. I've tried to put it behind me. I've tried to forget it. "

"If I had known about it, I might have been able to help you work through it. I might have been more patient and understanding. I hope someday you'll be able to forgive my shortcomings."

"You didn't know, and I didn't know how to talk about it. There's nothing to forgive."

"You surely are wise for a 14-year-old," Mrs. Lockhart said.

"You have to grow up pretty fast when you lose your parents when you're five years old."

"I've learned a lot from you, especially in the last couple of weeks. I want you to know that you have made a big impression on me. I will be a better mother and a better foster mother next time because of you. Please write us a letter occasionally and let us know how you're doing – I mean, how you really are doing."

"Sure," I said. "Kathy and I have already made plans to write each other."

"And if there are things you just want to tell me, you can write me separately."

"Okay."

"Good morning, Miss Hurley," Mr. Lockhart said. I hadn't even heard the doorbell.

"She's early," I whispered. "I'll go tell Kathy 'bye and get my things."

Kathy and I hugged and cried. If I had left a month ago, it would have been a very different scene. Kathy was too upset to leave the bedroom.

When I returned to the living room, I was surprised to see Miss Hurley with a suitcase in her hand. "Are you going on a trip?" I asked.

"No, Lorraine," she said. "The suitcase is for you."

I gently put down the half-full grocery bag I was clutching to my chest and approached Miss Hurley.

"Thank you," I said. "I've never had a suitcase. It's beautiful." I ran my hands over the suitcase and admired every hinge and clasp. It was a beautiful shade of red. I set it down on the sofa and opened it. It had a new smell. "This must have cost you a fortune, Miss Hurley."

"I can't take credit for the suitcase," Miss Hurley said. "A nearby church collected suitcases for foster children after they heard that most foster children only have a paper bag in which to pack their belongings. Someone who doesn't even know you bought this and wanted you to have it."

"I'd like to thank them," I said.

"Don't worry," Miss Hurley said. "I already have."

"Why don't you go to your bedroom and transfer your things to the suitcase?" Mrs. Lockhart asked. "That way, you can pack without an audience."

I appreciated her thoughtfulness. After all, a 14-year-old girl doesn't want to pack her underwear in front of her father, even her temporary foster dad. Kathy was in the bathroom, so I had the bedroom all to myself. I thought about leaving the grocery bag behind, but then I thought I'd better keep it. I thought I might need it later, in case something happened to my suitcase. Everything I owned fit into the suitcase with lots of room to spare. I left the suitcase on my bed and went to the living room.

"Is something wrong?" Mrs. Lockhart asked.

"Not exactly," I said. "It's just that the suitcase is too big. I could use a smaller one, if you have one. Another foster kid might need the big one."

"Keep this one," Miss Hurley said. "Maybe someday you'll fill it up."

"Okay," I said. "I just wanted to make sure." With that, I went and got my suitcase and started down the hall. I thought I heard Kathy crying. She was still in the bathroom. I stopped for a few seconds to take control of my emotions. The last time I left a sister crying in the bathroom, I never saw her again. I thought about telling Kathy goodbye again, but then I thought better of it. It would just make both of us cry harder.

Mrs. Lockhart bragged on how confident and grown up I looked when I entered the living room carrying my suitcase.

"It took me a little while to figure out how to open and close it," I said. "I love it! I feel like a real person – not a throwaway child."

"It's amazing what something as simple as a suitcase can do," Mr. Lockhart said.

"Well, I guess it's time for us to be on our way," Miss Hurley said.

I hugged Mr. Lockhart and thanked him for all he had done for me. He tried to speak, but his jaw trembled and he was not able to say anything.

Mrs. Lockhart was already crying when I turned to hug her. "Let us hear from you," she said. "We don't want to lose track of you."

I heard Miss Hurley open the front door behind me. Mrs. Lockhart held me at arm's length and then we had another quick hug. She kissed me on the forehead.

"I love y'all," I said as I looked at Mr. and Mrs. Lockhart. I grabbed the handle of my suitcase and hurried out the door before I lost my nerve to leave.

Miss Hurley and I had a quiet hour's drive to my new foster home. I was apprehensive about meeting my new temporary parents, but being able to walk into their house with a suitcase made all the difference in the world. I would never think of myself as a throwaway child again.

As soon as Mr. and Mrs. Hampton opened the door and welcomed Miss Hurley and me into their home, I knew everything was going to be all right. Like I told you in the beginning, I am pretty good at reading adults.

Author's Note:

A few years ago, the Witness and Service Committee at Rocky River Presbyterian Church in Cabarrus County, North Carolina, contacted the Department of Social Services (DSS) to get ideas for a possible mission project. When word came back that they were sorely in need of suitcases for foster children, we knew we had a project we could get exited about.

We were told that many foster children show up at their foster homes with their belongings stuffed in a garbage bag. The supervisor said that it made some of the children feel like they were "throw away kids." Our congregation enthusiastically donated gently-used and new suitcases – enough to supply the foster children in our county for about a year.

The DSS supervisor's words and the image of precious, frightened, and distraught children having nothing but a garbage bag to put their belongings in has stuck with me for years and inspired me to write this short story. Also, a friend of mine and her husband adopted two little girls whose mother had died in a house fire.

All the names in the story are fictitious.

Ghost of the Battle of Guilford Courthouse

Greensboro, North Carolina
1965

We'd been in our dream house in Guilford County, North Carolina for three days when the nightmares started. Our six-year-old daughter, Madison, ran into our bedroom in the middle of the night screaming, "There's a man in my room!" Her border collie-corgi mixed dog, Bandit, was at her heels. Madison landed in the middle of our bed.

My husband, Larry, leapt out of bed and dashed barefoot down the hall to Madison's room. "Come on, Bandit," he yelled as he grabbed a golf club to use as a weapon.

I turned on the bedside lamp. "You must have had a bad dream," I said, but Madison could not be consoled. All the news reports of child abductions ran through my head as I nervously patted Madison's head, which was now under the covers. I listened for any signs of distress from Larry. I contemplated calling 911. My free hand alternated between the phone on the nightstand and Madison's trembling shoulder. The digital clock on the nightstand read 3:15. Just then a flash of lightning lit up the room. It was followed immediately by a crack of thunder. Madison tightened her grip on my body.

In between claps of thunder, I could hear Larry moving throughout the house, opening and closing closet doors.

Madison's violent trembling made the entire bed shake.

"There's no one here but us," Larry said, when he and Bandit returned to our bedroom. "It was just a bad dream. You can go back to bed now. Bandit and I checked every room, every closet, and under your bed. There's no one here but us."

Madison still sobbed. Her head came out from under the covers. As soon as Larry got to the bed, Madison jumped into his arms. "But he was there, Daddy! At the foot of my bed." She buried her face in his pajama shirt.

"You must have had a nightmare, honey," Larry said. "I've checked your room and the whole house. There's no one here but the three of us. If a man had come into your room, Bandit would have barked. Bandit didn't wake you up, did he?"

"No, I just woke up and there he was." Madison's lower lip quivered and she fought to stop the tears that welled up in her eyes.

"Daddy's right," I said. "You know Bandit would have barked. It was a bad dream. I'll take you back to bed."

"Will you stay until I go back to sleep, Mom?" Madison asked as hand-in-hand we returned to her princess-style pink bedroom. I couldn't help but wonder if one of the Prince Charmings from the posters on her wall had intruded her dreams and become too real. Madison clung to her favorite stuffed bear and soon drifted off to sleep. I stepped over a whimpering Bandit and tiptoed back to my bedroom.

At 4 a.m. I was startled out of a deep sleep by the sensation of a man standing at the foot of our bed. I gasped and sat straight up in bed. He was already gone. My heart pounded. By the light of the hall night light, I could see Bandit standing in the doorway, his tail curled between his legs, his ears slicked back.

"Not you, too?" Larry grumbled, and then he rolled over and went back to sleep.

"What is it, Bandit?" I whispered, but he growled and trotted back toward Madison's room.

I mumbled something to myself about the power of suggestion, and after a few minutes went back to sleep.

A couple of hours later, Madison complained of a stomach ache and refused to eat breakfast. She was out-of-sorts from lack of sleep.

"You believe me, don't you, Mom?" she asked. "About that man being in my room last night."

"I believe you really think you saw him. Sometimes we can have a dream that's so vivid or real we're tricked into thinking it really happened."

"This really did happen. Nobody believes me." Madison stomped out the door to meet the school bus.

***

When I got home from the office that evening, everything looked normal until I opened the pantry door to get something to cook for dinner. There was a can of peaches lying on the floor. When I reached to picked it up, I saw several drops of dried blood on the vinyl flooring. Larry must have cut himself this morning and knocked the peaches off the shelf. Not like him to leave it there.

I put the can back on the shelf, wiped up the blood with a damp paper towel, and forgot about it. I peeled potatoes and put them on the stove to boil. A few minutes later the upstairs commode flushed. I figured Madison was upstairs, so I thought nothing of it until a second later when she came into the kitchen and asked me to help her with a word she had trouble reading. I pronounced the word for her, syllable by syllable.

"Were you just upstairs in the bathroom?" I asked as she turned to go.

"No, ma'am. I've just been in the den since we got home."

"Did you flush the commode downstairs?"

"No, Mom." She returned to the den.

I turned down the burner on the stove and crept up the stairs. My heart pounded in my chest and ears. I eased the hall closet door open and grasped Larry's old baseball bat. If I found someone in the house I wanted to surprise them. I knew I could do some damage with the bat.

I looked in each room as I came to it and checked every closet and window. There was no one there and all the windows were locked. I wondered if I had imagined hearing the flushing commode. Perhaps it had a slow leak and I heard the tank refill.

***

That night the three of us slept all night without any wild dreams or bedroom visitors, but at 3:15 a.m. the following night Madison came running into our room screaming with Bandit leading the way. Had Bandit seen or heard something, or had he been startled by Madison?

"That man's in my room again, Daddy!" she managed to say between sobs. She buried her head under the comforter on our bed as Larry went to check things out.

This was happening too often. It was getting tiring. I wanted to believe Madison was having a recurring nightmare, but I had a feeling in my gut that there was something more to it than that.

Again, Larry found no one in the house. He returned to our bedroom and propped his trusty nine iron in the corner.

"Since it's already getting light outside, let's go downstairs for pancakes," I said.

Madison and I went downstairs hand-in-hand. She sat down at the table and laid her head on her crossed arms. "I'm sleepy," she said.

"I'm sure you are. You aren't getting enough sleep thanks to those dreams you're having. Take a nap while I cook the pancakes."

I opened the pantry door and flipped the light switch. There on the floor were a can of peaches and five bright red drops of blood. I instinctively looked up. That's what watching too many horror movies will do for a person! When I saw no signs of blood dripping from anywhere in the pantry, I felt silly for looking at the ceiling. There had to be a logical explanation for this. I just didn't know what it was. I left the can and the blood droplets alone this time, grabbed the box of pancake mix and bottle of maple syrup off the shelf, and closed the door.

Madison loved pancakes and I thought doing something out of the ordinary for breakfast might take her mind off her nightmares. That turned out to be wishful thinking. Madison played with her pancakes and got on the school bus with a granola bar in her hand and a promise to eat it on the way to school. I did no better, not able to get my mind off the blood in the pantry.

"It's beginning to affect her eating habits," I said, when Larry came in with the morning's *Greensboro News & Record*. "We've got to do something."

"Don't panic yet," Larry said. "It's probably her brain's way of dealing with the move. I think the nightmares will stop when she get accustomed to her new surroundings." He folded the newspaper and laid it on the kitchen table.

"I suppose you're right."

"Did you sleep okay last night?"

"Yes, until Bandit and Madison woke me up."

"Yeah, me, too."

"I need to show you something," I said. I got up and started toward the pantry door. "Come here. You've got to see this."

Larry rolled his eyes but got up from the table and followed me. I opened the pantry door and pointed to the floor.

"What caused that?" he asked.

"If I knew, I wouldn't have left it for you to see. The same thing happened day before yesterday. When I came home from work, the same can of peaches and three drops of blood were in that same place. And that night while I cooked dinner, the upstairs commode flushed. I thought it was Madison, but she was in the den. I'm beginning to get spooked. What are we going to do?"

"I'll get a camera," Larry said. "Right now I can't think of anything else to do, can you?'

"No. I don't like to feel this way. I don't believe in ghosts, but this scares me. What does he want?"

"I'm just guessing, but I'd say peaches," Larry said. His face lit up in a silly grin.

"Not funny," I said, but I couldn't help but laugh. "This is serious. There's blood on the floor. Madison's not able to eat or sleep. We have to do something. We have to get rid of whatever this is."

Larry picked up his cell

"Who are you calling?"

"Ghost busters!" he said.

"Very funny!" This time I didn't laugh. "Maybe he'll wake you up next time. You won't laugh then."

***

The coming weeks were filled with our busy schedules at work and Madison's school activities. There were PTO meetings, parent-teacher conferences, and soccer games. About once a week, Madison would have the recurring nightmares, and then I started having them again, too. It usually happened at 3:15 a.m.

Several mornings as I packed Madison's lunch box I was sure someone had walked up behind me, but I turned around and found no one there. Sometimes I was sure I heard the upstairs commode flush when the three of us were downstairs watching TV. Madison didn't seem to notice, but Larry and I would exchange quizzical glances.

Occasionally, a neighbor would ask Larry or me if we'd seen the ghost yet. "No, we haven't seen any ghosts," was our standard reply. Neither of us believed in ghosts and we were embarrassed to admit there was something unexplainable going on in our house.

Then one night, we both became believers. It was about 3:15 on a Sunday morning. Larry and I had both had a stressful week at work and one or the other of us had a meeting every night. Saturday we cleaned the house and worked in the yard until we were ready to drop.

"I think I'll sleep well tonight," I said as I turned off my bedside lamp. "Stay up and read if you want. Your light won't bother me. I'm too exhausted for anything to bother me. I don't know why I bothered to set the alarm clock. It will take an explosion to wake me in the morning."

I was asleep before my head hit the pillow, but it was not to last. At 3:15 that night Madison and Bandit came running into our bedroom. Madison took a flying leap and landed in the middle of our bed. Poor Bandit's short corgi legs made it impossible for him to jump on the bed, so he dived under it. As Larry got up to perform his obligatory room-by-room house check, Bandit's snout came out from under the dust ruffle. There came a bass growl so low it sounded like it came up from the dog's toenails as Larry sped past and out the door.

"Get out!" I heard Larry yell from downstairs.

I jumped out of bed and ran to the bedroom door to lock it, and then I grabbed my cell and dialed 911. Just as the emergency dispatcher answered, I heard Larry's footsteps in the hall.

"Just a moment," I said to the dispatcher.

"Ma'am, are you having an emergency?"

"I'm not sure. Just a minute." I turned my head away from the phone. "Should I unlock the door, Larry?"

"Yes, there's no one here."

I opened the bedroom door. Larry looked like he'd seen a ghost. "Are you all right? You don't look so good."

"Do you need assistance, ma'am?" the dispatcher asked. I detected a twinge of urgency in her voice that time, or was it frustration?

"No, I don't think we do. I'm sorry I called. We thought there was an intruder downstairs, but my husband didn't find anyone."

"That's good, ma'am," the dispatcher said. "We'll be glad to send a patrol car out. It might be a good idea to have an officer look around."

"Do you want them to send someone?" I asked Larry.

He shook his head.

"No, that won't be necessary," I said. "Thank you for your patience. I was scared."

"You're welcome. That's what we're here for."

I disconnected the call and helped Larry to the bed. He sat down and Madison snuggled up under his arm.

"Who were you talking to downstairs, Daddy?" she asked.

"No one, honey. There was no one there. I thought there was at first, but I was mistaken. There's no one here but the three of us. Go back to bed, sweetheart."

I gave Larry a hard look. I knew he'd seen something that he didn't want to discuss in front of Madison, so I took her back to her room and tucked her in. I sat on the side of her bed until she fell asleep. I was so tired, I nearly drifted off. I caught myself just as I started to fall. I stumbled back to our room and crawled into bed.

"Are you sure you're all right?" I asked Larry.

"Yeah, I'm okay. Goodnight again."

"What did you see downstairs?"

"Nothing. It had to be nothing. Goodnight."

"I can see you aren't ready to tell me. Goodnight." I was soon asleep.

When the alarm went off several hours later, Larry was sitting up in bed. He stared off in space and looked like I imagined zombies look.

"You surely slept well," Larry said. There was an edge of envy in his voice.

"Yes, I did. Should I apologize?

"No."

"Why do you sound disgusted with me?"

"Because I haven't slept since Madison woke us up. I don't know how to tell you this, but there was a man sitting at our kitchen table when I went down to check on things."

"A man in our kitchen?" I jumped out of bed and stared at Larry in disbelief. I didn't know whether to be mad at him for not telling me when he came upstairs or to be scared. "Why didn't you tell me? Why didn't you let me have the dispatcher send the police?"

"Because as soon as I said, 'Get out,' he vanished into thin air."

"Vanished? You mean, like a ghost?"

"Yeah, that pretty well describes it."

"What did he look like?" I sat down on the bed and took Larry's hand in mine.

"He wore a red coat, like you see British soldiers wearing in artists' drawings of the Revolutionary War. He looked to be around 25 years old, clean-shaven, with brown hair in a kind of pony tail at the nape of his neck."

"That's it! I've been trying to figure out how the man is dressed. Yes! He's a Revolutionary War soldier! I saw him in a dream later that night after Madison's first nightmare, but when I woke up I couldn't piece the details together."

"His bayonet was propped in the corner between the pantry door and the refrigerator."

"Yewwww! Bayonet?"

"Well, he is a soldier."

"Come to think of it, he carried a rifle or musket when I saw him in my dream."

"There's something unique about him," Larry said.

"You don't think a man dressed like a Revolutionary War British soldier sitting at our kitchen table in the middle of the night is unique?"

"I mean, he wasn't just any soldier. His right coat sleeve was bloody and hung limp. There was no hand at the end of the sleeve. He appeared to have only one arm."

"Maybe he lost it in the war."

"He must have. Surely, he wouldn't have been drafted into the army that way."

"That's a good point." We laughed.

"I can't believe how matter-of-factly we're discussing this," Larry said.

"Me, too. You said he was sitting at the table. What was he doing?"

"He was sitting there at my place staring at a can of peaches."

I gasped and my hand flew to cover my gapping mouth.

"Are you thinking what I'm thinking?" Larry asked.

"We need to look for that can of peaches, don't we?"

"Uh-huh."

I slipped on my bedroom shoes and robe and followed Larry downstairs. He turned on the light and we crept into the kitchen. There on the table was a can of peaches!

"Tell me you put them there," I said.

"No, I didn't."

"We only have one can of peaches. Every day it has more dents in the rim from falling off the shelf."

"Or from being dropped," Larry said. "Show me where you put it this morning."

Larry stepped aside to allow me passage into the walk-in closet that served as our pantry. I reached behind several rows of canned vegetables to where I had put the peach can that morning. "There's nothing there! It's gone!"

We stood there for a minute staring at the dented can of peaches in Larry's hand. "Here," he said. "Put it back there again. Let's see how long this goes on. There's no way it can fall off the shelf."

I put the can on the back of the shelf, turned out the pantry light, and closed the door.

"Are you sure you don't believe in ghosts?" Larry asked.

"Yes, I'm sure. I've never put any stock in ghost stories. What about you?"

"No. I've always thought people who believed in ghosts were a little unstable."

"Do you think we're unstable?" I asked, only half in jest.

"I don't know what to think," Larry said."

Just then, I heard Madison and Bandit bouncing down the stairs. Bandit went straight to his water bowl and Madison rubbed the sleep from her eyes.

"Is that man with the long gun going to come into my room again tonight?" Madison asked.

"The man has a long gun?" I asked. Madison had never mentioned a gun.

"Uh-huh," she said. "He's dressed funny, too. He doesn't wear long pants like Daddy. His pants stop at his knees. And he wears a bright red coat."

"Could you draw a picture of him?" Larry asked.

"Sure," Madison said.

I put a piece of paper on the kitchen table and opened the plastic box in which she kept an array of crayons. She immediately set to work. Larry and I sat down at the table and watched her work. It was obvious she knew in detail the image she wanted to portray. She drew a line out from the man's mouth and scribbled the name 'Mary' inside the circle. She finished and handed the drawing to us. It was a remarkable drawing of the man I had seen.

"That's perfect!" Larry said. "I can't believe what a good job you did. I have a question, though. Why did you only draw one arm on the man?"

"Because he only has one arm."

"And why did you write the name 'Mary' coming from his mouth?" I asked.

"Because that's the name he always says. It's like he's looking for a girl named Mary, but he says it funny."

"How does he say it?" I asked.

"He says it more like, oh, I can't say it like he does. It's like the way you've told me people in Scotland say an 'r.'"

"Have you heard him talk?" Larry asked me as Madison skipped off to the bathroom.

"No, but there's no doubt in Madison's mind. Right down to his Scottish accent."

"Even though he frightens her when he appears to her in the night, she very calmly drew his picture."

"That's right. Come to think of it, I don't feel threatened by him. It's creepy, but I don't think he wants to hurt us."

***

The neighborhood cookout and get-acquainted party was that afternoon. I tried to figure out how to broach the subject of ghosts with these strangers. The usual nervous small talk took place before the burgers were ready. Conversation ran the gamut from, "How many children do you have?" to "What do you do for a living?" and "Where did you move here from?" By the time the children's plates were served and the adults sat down to eat, I felt more at ease. I opened my mouth to say, "I don't believe in ghosts, but" when our next door neighbor, Claire, asked, "Is anyone getting a full night's sleep yet?"

"No!" blurted Avery from across the street. "My husband says he's about ready to put our house on the market."

"My feelings, exactly," added Shelley from the next block. "Once in a while we get to sleep all night, but not often. I'm not scared, but this is getting old."

"I don't believe in ghosts," I said, "but some strange things wake us up in the middle of the night. Does a Revolutionary War soldier appear at the foot of your bed?"

"We call him the 'Welcome Wagon," Shelley said.

"We call him 'Friar Tuck' at our house," Gail said. "He never scares me or makes me feel uneasy. I sort of like having him around, but it's been my experience that house guests are slow to warm up to him."

"Your guests have seen him?" I asked.

"Oh, yes. My sister-in-law came one weekend. She turned in early in our spare bedroom. A few minutes later she flew downstairs and asked if I had just been in her room. I told her I hadn't, and she said she could have sworn someone had come into her room, stood at the foot of the bed, and called her by name."

"What name was that?" I asked. My heart beat faster as I anticipated the answer.

"Her name is Mary."

"That's interesting," I said. "Our daughter has been waked up repeatedly by nightmares. She thinks there's a man in her room saying the name "Mary" in a Scottish accent. She drew a picture of him for us this morning. He's dressed like a British soldier from the Revolutionary War."

"That's him," Shelley said. "Just wait until he starts dropping cans of peaches in your kitchen."

"Or leaving drops of blood around the house," Claire said.

"I can't believe y'all! There's no such thing as a ghost," I said, but my voice was shaky.

"Are you trying to convince us or yourself?" Shelley asked.

"I don't believe in ghosts," I said.

"You're a little too emphatic," Claire said.

The other women laughed. My face burned in embarrassment. I knew I'd given myself away, but I couldn't bring myself to admit I'd seen a ghost.

***

We all enjoyed a good night's sleep that night. I thought maybe "Friar Tuck" had heard the afternoon's conversation and been scared off. Over breakfast, after Madison had left for school, Larry said having a soldier in the house had given him an idea.

"You don't plan to join the army, do you?" I asked.

"No," he said, almost spewing coffee from his mouth. "Don't be ridiculous. The army wouldn't have me."

"Okay. What's your idea?"

"I want us to take Madison to the Guilford Courthouse National Military Park on Saturday. We need to learn all we can about our new neighborhood and city."

"Sounds good to me. Let's do it."

***

Madison was immediately captivated by the exhibits at the Park's visitors' center.

"Mom! Daddy! It's him!" Madison called out. We were several steps behind her in the exhibit hall. "It's the man who's been coming in my room!"

"That's the way he was dressed," Larry whispered in my direction.

"Read what it says, Daddy," Madison said. She pulled on Larry's hand with one hand and pointed to the exhibit with the other.

I read along silently as Larry read the words to Madison. "'The following words are from a diary kept by John Stewart, a soldier in the British Brigade of Guards. The Brigade of Guards was one of the units of the British Army engaged in the Battle of Guilford Courthouse on March 15, 1781.'"

"March 15 would translate to 3:15," I said. "Kind of eery that's the time we're usually awakened."

Larry shrugged and continued to read aloud. "It says here, 'March 14, 1781. My name is John Stewart. I was born in Scotland and raised on a croft. When I was 17 years old, all my family except for me died with the plague. I had no way to survive there with no rights to the land and no living kinfolk, so I set out for Greenock where I got a job loading and unloading ships. It was in Greenock that I met Mary."

"Did you say, 'Mary'?" Madison asked. "That's the name the man in my bedroom keeps saying. This is the right soldier!"

"Sure sounds like it," I said.

"It says here," Larry said, "that they were going to get married, but the army came to town and pressed him into service. That's how he ended up in America."

"What else does it say?" Madison asked.

"'We fought at the Cowpens in South Carolina and then came up to Hillsborough in North Carolina. We've marched so much that my blisters have blisters. I don't like what we've been doing, but they'll shoot you if you don't follow orders. We burned Rev. Hugh McAden's papers and then we were ordered to plunder at Buffalo Presbyterian Church. It nearly killed me when we were ordered to burn Rev. David Caldwell's books and papers at Alamance Presbyterian. These people have Scottish names. It's like I'm being told to kill my own people.

"We're camped tonight near Guilford Courthouse, and we've been told to prepare ourselves for battle tomorrow. I don't take any enjoyment from battle, but it's cold tonight and I'd rather be doing most anything other than sitting and thinking. They keep us busy marching and drilling most days; they say to keep us ready to fight. I think they do it to wear us out so we'll be too tired to fight each other. It's boring and I hate it. If I had wanted to be a soldier, I would've joined the army when I left the croft. I didn't want to sleep on the cold, wet ground. All I wanted was to live out my life with Mary and our children, but here I sit, shivering on a rock, unable to think of anything except how cold it is and how homesick I am for Mary. That's why I started writing this. I know nobody will ever read this, but I just wanted to write down my thoughts. I have a really bad feeling in my gut about that battle tomorrow.'"

"What happened the next day?" Madison asked.

"It tells about the movements of the armies the next morning," Larry said. "General Nathanael Greene commanded the Americans."

"I don't think you're interested in the military details," I said, placing my hand on Madison's shoulders. I guided her around the corner to the next display. While we waited for Larry to catch up with us, Madison and I looked at artifacts found on the battlefield. There were wood-handled forks, a tin tinderbox, leather canteens, tin cups with handles, and a powder horn on which the 18th century owner had etched a map showing the various battles in which he had fought. There were muskets and rifles, one with a bayonet attached.

"That's the kind of gun the man in my dreams has," Madison said, pointing to the rifle with the bayonet. "It's scary!" She squeezed my hand.

Larry walked up beside me.

"What happened to Mr. Stewart?" Madison asked. "Does it say?"

"Let's see," said Larry. "It says, 'British soldier, John Stewart, apparently had a premonition because he met his death the next afternoon at the Battle of Guilford Courthouse. Unfortunately for John Stewart, fate place him at the end of the broadsword of the famous patriot, Peter Francisco.'"

I touched Larry's arm and shook my head, pointing to the display sign with my eyes. He read on silently and soon discovered why I had stopped him in mid-paragraph.

"What's it say?" Madison asked. "Did Peter Francisco kill Mr. Stewart with his sword?"

Larry stammered for a few seconds. I knew he didn't want to tell our daughter how Francisco slew 11 Brits, including splitting John Stewart's buddy's head down to his shoulders.

"It says that Peter Francisco was known as 'The Goliath of the Revolution' because he was such a big man," Larry said. "Most men in the 1700s were not as tall and big as we are today because we have better food to eat today. We have more variety and we know about vitamins and nutrition that they didn't know about then. It says Peter Francisco was six-feet-six inches tall and weighed 260 pounds. That's a hundred pounds more than I weight and seven inches taller than I am." Larry demonstrated with his hands how much larger Peter Francisco was then himself.

"So what does it say Peter Francisco did in the battle?" Madison asked.

"It says he killed 11 British soldiers, and he cut one soldier's arm off," Larry said.

"Was it John Stewart?" Madison asked. Her eyes filled with tears.

"Yes," I said. "I'm afraid he did."

"What happened to Mr. Stewart then?" she asked.

"It says he was taken to the New Garden Meeting House where he was cared for by Quakers."

"Did he get all right?" Madison asked.

"It says that the British evacuated the area on March 18th, leaving behind 64 wounded soldiers, including John Stewart," Larry said. "The British marched off toward Cross Creek, which is now called Fayetteville, and eventually to Virginia where they surrendered to the Americans at Yorktown."

"But what about Mr. Stewart? He only had one arm. What happened to him?" Madison asked.

"It says he died at the New Garden Meeting House. I'm sorry," I said.

Madison started to cry. "I didn't want him to die!" she said. She stomped her feet in protest.

"Wait a minute," I said. "Look at this next part. It says that John Stewart's spirit lives on today in Guilford County. It says, "For years he was seen wandering the battlefield in search of his arm. For decades, he continued to walk the dirt roads of the county. It is said that he has taken shelter in various houses and farm outbuildings over the last two centuries. Early in the 21st century, as more houses have been built to accommodate the growing population, many people have reported feeling the presence of Mr. Stewart in their home. It is thought he is looking for his one true love, Mary. He seems to have an affinity for peaches, a fruit he wouldn't have tasted until he came to the American South."

The three of us stood for several minutes at the exhibit.

Madison broke the silence. "I feel sorry for Mr. Stewart. He lost his arm and he's homesick for Mary, but I don't want him to live in our house."

"I don't either," I said. "Let's go home and see what we can come up with now that we know his story."

"What would you like for lunch?" I asked Madison as I took her hand and we walked to the car.

"A hamburger and fries," she said. "And could we have peaches for dessert?"

"Yes, we can," I said. "I believe there's a can in the pantry."

***

After lunch the three of us sat around the kitchen table. "We need a plan," Larry said. He winked at me. "I believe Mr. Stewart is looking for two things here. He's looking for peaches and he's looking for his arm. We just ate the only peaches in the house, right?"

"Yes," I said.

"I say we make a sign that says we have no peaches and put it in the pantry," Larry said.

"But what about his arm?" Madison said. "We don't have an extra arm to give him."

"I have a friend who works at Belk," I said. "I'll ask her if we can get an arm from a mannequin. A mannequin is what they put clothes on in the stores so you can see what they will look like on a real person. We can put it in the pantry. Maybe Mr. Stewart will take it, read the sign, and leave us alone."

"It's worth a try," Madison said.

We put our plan in place that afternoon. Larry and Madison made a poster board sign. I called my friend at the store, and she brought us a mannequin's arm that night. Larry and I were awakened by a noise downstairs around three o'clock the next morning. We tiptoed down the hall past Madison's bedroom. We found Bandit at the top of the stairs, cocking his head from side-to-side as if he were hearing noises, too. It sounded like someone moving cans around in the pantry.

"I guess he doesn't believe the sign," I said. Larry and I chuckled to ourselves. Then it grew quiet. After a few minute of silence, we crept down the stairs. There were several drops of blood on the poster board sign, and the mannequin's arm was gone. I shivered and squeezed Larry's arm more tightly.

"I don't believe this," Larry said.

"Neither do I," I said. "It was just a ploy to convince Madison that the ghost was gone. I didn't expect the arm to be taken. I told Kay I'd give it back to her in a few days. Kay had laughed about the whole things. She said I was silly to go along with Madison's nightmares. She said we were carrying this too far."

"Now what are you going to tell her?"

"I don't know. I don't think she'll believe the truth."

"But Madison will, and that's the important thing."

The next morning while Madison was eating her cereal, Larry and I sat down at the kitchen table with her.

"We think Mr. Stewart is gone," Larry said.

"What makes you think that?" Madison asked.

"Look in the pantry," I said, as I got up. I walked to the pantry door, opened it, and turned on the light. Madison craned her neck to look.

"The sign is gone," she said. She came stood beside me. She leaned her head into the pantry. "What happened to the arm?"

"It's gone," I said. "Your dad, Bandit, and I heard noises down here during the night. When we came downstairs, the arm was gone."

"Cool!" Madison said.

"It looks like our plan worked," Larry said.

"I hope Mr. Stewart likes his new arm," Madison said. "Maybe now he can find his way back to Scotland to Mary."

"Maybe so," I said.

Two years have passed since our last visit from John Stewart. I still hesitate to bring canned peaches into the house, and I guess I always will. Madison mentions Mr. Stewart from time-to-time, but she hasn't seen him in her bedroom any more. I look for blood droplets every time I go into the pantry. I can't seem to erase that one-armed soldier from my mind. The neighbors still see him occasionally. They say he drops his new arm sometimes while rummaging through their canned fruits, but he always picks it up and takes it with him. I haven't told them where he got the arm. They say he still calls out for his beloved Mary. I'm not going to tell Madison.

Author's Note: I've never believed in ghosts, but this story is based on the events my sister and her housemate experienced in their condominium in Greensboro, North Carolina in the 1980s. The upstairs commode would flush when no one was upstairs. Cans occasionally fell of the pantry shelf. A house guest was frightened by the sensation that someone had walked into her bedroom and stood at the foot of her bed. In fact, she thought this person had called her by name: Mary. She had no knowledge of the unexplained incidents the residents had experienced.

Peter Francisco was an actual American soldier in the Battle of Guilford Courthouse. At six-feet-six inches tall and 260 pounds, he was much larger than the average American man during that era. He was credited with being ruthless with his broadsword.

There is a visitors' center on the grounds of the Battle of Guilford Courthouse; however, the rest of story is fiction.

IF THIS HOUSE COULD TALK

Cabarrus County, North Carolina

1975

I sit by the side of a road that is no more. If my walls and the red clay soil I sit on could speak, this is the story they would tell.

Archibald Smith bought the land I sit on today. I've seen happy times and I've seen sad times that would have destroyed a lesser man than Archie. More than 150 years have passed since Archie built me. My rusty tin roof has caved in, most of my window panes have cracked or been broken out, and my wooden walls and floors bow and sag.

My front porch looks out on a path that my current owner uses to transport his cattle and their hay from one pasture or barn to another. That path used to be a road that led over to the Snell place and Welch's Mill on McKee Creek. Francis Snell was one of the first, if not the first, teacher in this section. That was before my time, though, but I heard it said that he taught the orphaned Morrison children way back in the 1780s.

On their way home from taking their corn to the mill, men would stop by to sit and rock on the front porch with Archie. Those were some of my favorite times. I'd learn all about politics and the gossip about who in the community had gotten in trouble for "weaving in the saddle" after having too much to drink.

Life is slow and quiet now because I sit vacant, but when I was young and strong, there was never a dull moment on this farm. If you are quiet and listen long and hard enough, you just might hear the laughter of little children or the weeping of their mother when they were forever taken away by war. You might see Archie stealing away in the barn to grieve in private for his first and second wives and for the children who died too soon.

The only time everything was still and quiet was at night when the Smiths were sleeping or on Sundays when they piled in a wagon dressed in their finest clothes and went off to church. At least, that's what they did on Sundays if the roads weren't too muddy or Reedy Creek wasn't out of its banks. I heard Archie say that his ancestors came from Scotland and were steeped in Presbyterianism. Those Presbyterians believe in conducting their business and their personal lives decently and in order, and that's the way Archie lived his life. It was the example he gave his family and friends.

Forgive me for getting ahead of myself. I should start my story in the beginning during the happy times. Archie was born near Welch's Mill and took Rebecca Davis as his wife in 1822. He went to work building me – a handsome wood frame house for the large family he and Rebecca wanted. Archie was a wagon maker by trade. He settled in to ply his trade at home and farmed to supplement that income. Archie was, no doubt, already well-established in his trade before he married Rebecca at the ripe old age of 26.

Ah, Rebecca! She was a bonnie lass of 21 when she married Archie. She came to me as a nervous bride on October 19, 1822, but she was soon adding touches of color and bits of lace and ruffles here and there. Every house yearns for a woman's touch and I was no exception. I let out a big sigh of relief and settled down to concentrate on my job, which was to keep Archie and his bride safe, dry, and warm.

Rebecca, Archie, and I gradually got into a routine that first fall and winter. Rebecca planted daffodil bulbs she brought from her mother's flower garden. Archie cut wood for cooking and heating and set aside logs suitable for making wagons. He had wagon building and repairing to do all along for people in the community. Rainy days kept him working on wagons in the barn. Sunny days found him clearing land for the next year's crops and a garden. As cold weather set in, Rebecca stayed busy cooking, washing, and ironing clothes.

By the time Rebecca's daffodils started blooming, I suspected that my happy young couple were going to become a family of three. Rebecca seemed unwell in the early mornings, and she often spent her afternoons knitting baby clothes.

Archie had a newfound spring in his step and set to work to have a showplace of a farm. He whistled while he worked and was ever so careful with Rebecca. When she kneeled to plant flowers in the spring or attempted to tend her garden during the hot, humid days of June and July, Archie would come running, help her to her feet, and try to do the work for her.

"You don't know how to space and group the flowers," Rebecca would say. "That's not how I wanted them."

"You're going to hurt yourself," Archie would answer. "You can plant them the way you want them next year."

My suspicions were confirmed on September 17, 1823, when Rebecca gave birth to a baby boy. They named him Johnathan D. Smith. I knew what the "D" stood for at the time, but that detail has long since been forgotten. It was possibly Davis – his mother's maiden name, but don't quote me on that.

As of Johnathan's birth, life as I had known it was over. It was hard to get any rest. Who knew that a baby could cry so much and scream so loudly? Suddenly, Rebecca and Archie were tired all the time. They loved that baby and talked to him in what I came to call "baby talk." I'd never seen Archie's silly side before, but that precious baby boy brought it out of him. Grandparents, aunts, uncles, and cousins came to visit often after the baby's arrival. The women always brought food.

I think Archie was afraid Rebecca would forget how to cook, but she was ever so grateful for every morsel that was brought in.

Archie had nothing to fear. Rebecca was her own person and she was eager to cook for her family and provide a cheerful and loving home for Archie and their son as soon as she felt like herself again.

I adored wee Johnathan. After he outgrew his incessant crying – I think his stomach hurt -- he brought much laughter to my walls. Three years later he would get a little sister. Her name was Margaret Rebecca, just like her sweet mother. The little family was perfect, although there was plenty of room in me for more children. Life was grand for a little while, but wee Margaret Rebecca was a sickly baby and didn't live very long. Then, much to my horror, the babe's mother died just four months after giving life to the infant.

Archie was distraught. He spent his days working on wagons and trying to keep an eye on Johnathan. There wasn't any laughter on the farm for a long time, and Johnathan and Archie both cried themselves to sleep for weeks. Fortunately, Johnathan was fascinated by his father's skills as a wagonmaker and a farmer, so he rarely strayed too far. But Johnathan needed a mother and Archie needed the affection and companionship of a wife.

He knew a lady named Sarah McClellan from church, and soon an attraction grew between them. Fearing she'd die without ever finding a life partner, Sarah was eager to get married at the age of 31 and longed to have a house full of children. She and Archie were married on December 29, 1831. It was so nice to have a woman here on the farm again!

Sarah loved Johnathan like his first mother did. He forever missed his birth mother, but he came to love Sarah with all his heart. She was a much better cook than his father, and put her special, gentle touch on things. Once again, I wasn't just a house. I was a home.

It wasn't long until Sarah started showing all the signs that another baby was coming. Catherine was born in September 1832. She had just learned how to walk her wobbly little baby walk when it became clear that another baby was on the way. Hugh was born in 1834.

I soon realized that my responsibilities were growing at a rapid pace. Will was born the next year, and he was followed by Jane in 1837. Eli was close behind in 1839, and Isaac came along in 1840. It was a good thing Archie had one of those family Bibles that had the extra pages between the Old and New Testaments for people to write down marriages, births, and deaths. Otherwise, I'm not sure he could have kept up with all his children's ages.

The county established a public school system in 1841, and the older children started going to school as they got old enough. I heard it said that the school only had one room and all the children studied in that one room no matter how old they were. That sounds like trouble to me because I remember what it was like when all the Smith children were in one room. It could get pretty noisy – laughing and having a good time one day and picking fights with each other the next.

There were two more children to come. Caroline in 1842, just missing Isaac's second birthday by four days. Last, but not least, Nathaniel came along to round out the family. I guess Archie was too busy and forgot to write Nathaniel's name in the family Bible. I can't recall the date now either, but I've been told that Mr. Joshua Harris, a noted record keeper in the community, jotted down that Nathaniel was baptized at the church in 1843. That sounds about right to me.

Now there were eight happy children in the house. Everything was going well until Sarah took sick and died in 1844. My oh my! Archie was beside himself with grief. I could tell he felt overwhelmed by the way he talked to God at night when he climbed into bed.

Johnathan was a mighty good help to his father. Although he was almost 22 years old when his step-mother died, he hadn't yet married. He still lived here with his father. Johnathan's little half-sister, Catherine, was not quite 12 years old at the time. Suddenly, she had to take on the duties of mother to her seven younger siblings. Trying to cook and clean for such a large family was more than even the most mature 11-year-old child could handle. I was relieved when various women in the extended family pitched in and gave Catherine and her seven younger brothers and sisters the support and attention they needed.

Having such a large, young family, Archie had little time to grieve for Sarah. He married a lady named Isabella in 1845. Isabella was a loving and caring woman. She moved to our farm and immediately went about the task of caring for Archie's heartbroken children. She didn't see it as a task, though. She loved children, and had none of her own.

With his father remarried and the family taken care of by Isabella, Johnathan felt free to seek a wife and life of his own. In preparation for Johnathan's marriage to Elizabeth Caldwell, he purchased 150 acres of land from Archie. That land was on the western end of Archie's farm and, according to the deed, began "at a post oak near the corner of Samuel Wilson's Orchard on the waters of Reedy and McKees Creek." That was a very old orchard. It was near the gristmill and was the reason Peach Orchard Road carries that name still today.

I think Archie was hesitant to get too attached to Isabella at first, for fear of losing her. Life on the farm fell into a routine again, though, and we all found a new normal. Archie's wagon business and farm flourished, and he bought additional land every few years. He bought 41 acres from an adjoining landowner in 1846. That property was crossed by Huggins Run.

In 1850, Archie purchased 22 acres of land on the banks of McKee Creek, and in 1850 he bought an additional 105 acres. I heard him tell Isabella that he was trying to accumulate enough acreage to offer some to each of his sons when they came of age. But the unfolding of history had other plans for the Smith family and the nation.

The first shots of the Civil War were fired on April 12, 1861 at Fort Sumter down in South Carolina. The news traveled fast from Charleston and within days the war was all the men talked about when they stopped by to visit Archie. Once again, there was no laughter within my walls. There were many tearful hugs goodbye as five of Archie's sons enlisted to fight for the duration of the war.

Eli enlisted on July 20, 1861 at the age of 22, leaving a pregnant wife behind. Will enlisted one week after Eli. Hugh enlisted on April 7, 1862 at the age of 27, leaving a wife and two small children behind.

Eli was killed near Goldsboro, North Carolina at a place called Ox Hill on September 1, 1863. He never got to see his precious daughter, Ella.

Isaac died in a "war camp" in March of 1863 at the age of 22.

Nathaniel was killed in the war and was buried somewhere in Virginia.

Hugh was wounded at Sharpsburg, Maryland in 1862, rejoined his company in the spring of 1863, and died of disease on November 10, 1863.

It should come as no surprise to anyone that Archie died on November 25, 1863, just 15 days after Hugh died. I will always believe that Archie died of a broken heart.

It is thought that Will was wounded near Richmond and got to come home with Dr. L.C. Kirkpatrick of Rocky River who had gone to Richmond after the seven days of battles there in June 1862 to tend to wounded soldiers from Cabarrus County. Dr. Kirkpatrick made arrangements for Will to come back home with him after the physician served there for seven days. Will died on November 25, 1866, exactly three years to the day after his father died.

The house felt empty after so much death. At night when all was quiet except for the mournful cries of a whippoorwill in the woods, I often heard Isabella's lonely footsteps as she roamed the house. She would occasionally bump into a chair or other piece of furniture as her eyesight failed. Not long after Archie's death, Isabella moved in with Archie and Sarah's daughter, Jane and her husband. I understand Isabella died in 1869.

Things never were the same. I thought when Sarah married Archie and they had so many healthy children that life was going to be perfect forevermore. My joy was short-lived. I try to think about the happy times and not dwell on the sad ones, but once the war started it seemed like there was nothing but sadness. A total of 72 men from the church were killed or died of disease in the war.

It was a long time after the war ended before I heard anyone laugh or saw anyone smile. I tried my best to keep my family safe. If only I could have kept them here on the farm and out of that horrible war....

More than 150 years have passed since that war. My floors sag and wind blows though the gaps in the old planks of my walls. Some of my window panes have been broken by accident, allowing birds to come in and nest in my rafters. I welcome the company. The land is still farmed. I hear the modern motorized tractors mowing hay for the cattle that graze behind me and across the dirt road, but the voices of children have disappeared.

I believe that someday this land will again be filled with the laughter of children.

Author's Note:

Until a few years ago, the Archibald Smith house stood less than a mile from where I grew up. I don't believe it was occupied anytime in my lifetime. It was a constant in my life. My family passed it every time we went to church. We usually passed it as my sister and I rode the school bus.

One thing that made an impression on me was that the house did not face the main road. It faced what was a driveway deeper into a large farm. That driveway is, no doubt, what remains of a colonial road. On occasion as we passed by in my childhood, my father would point past the house and say, "The old Snell place was back there."

"The old Snell place" meant nothing to me at the time. It was years later that I met a descendant of those Snells. It was years later that I learned from my fourth-great-grandfather's 1777 estate papers that Mr. Francis Snell was a teacher.

It was years later, when I researched the 72 men and boys from Rocky River Presbyterian Church in Cabarrus County, North Carolina, who were killed or died of disease during the American Civil War that I learned that Archibald Smith lost five sons in that horrible war. It was that fact that has stayed with me for the last several decades and, more than anything else, prompted me to write this story.

ABOUT THE AUTHOR

Janet Morrison grew up in Harrisburg, North Carolina. She holds a Bachelor of Arts degree in Political Science with a minor in History from Appalachian State University and a Master of Public Affairs from North Carolina State University at Raleigh. After a career in public administration, in 2001, Janet took a fiction writing course at Queens University of Charlotte. It led her in a new direction.

Since taking that writing class, Janet has written two local history books, historical short stories, a devotional book, and a journal to accompany the devotional book. All of those experiences and her blog have helped her find her writer's voice.

Janet started her blog, Janet's Writing Blog, in 2010. Janet blogs opinion pieces about current events, shares her thoughts about some of the books she reads, writes posts of historical significance on or near the anniversary dates of those events, and occasionally writes about local North Carolina history. Find her blog at https://www.janetswriting blog.com

Traveling Through History is Janet's first collection of original historical short stories. Two of the stories introduce you to characters who will show up in her planned series of historical novels set along The Great Wagon Road in Virginia, North Carolina, and South Carolina in the 1760s.

Her website is https://www.janetmorrisonbooks.com. Visit her website to subscribe to her newsletter. By doing so, you will receive a free downloadable copy of her historical short story, "Slip Sliding Away."

ALSO BY JANET MORRISON

Janet's first love is writing historical fiction, but her writing journey has meandered through a variety of books and writing experiences.

Most recently, before publishing this collection of historical short stories, Janet wrote a devotional book, *I Need The Light! 26 Weekly Devotionals to Help You Through Winter* and *I Need The Light! Companion Journal and Diary*, out of her decades of experience with Chronic Fatigue Syndrome, Fibromyalgia, and Seasonal Affective Disorder. She needs natural light in the mornings to combat Seasonal Affective Disorder, and she needs Jesus Christ — The Light of the World — to cope with all life's challenges and stresses.

As a freelance writer, Janet wrote a local history column for *Harrisburg Horizons* newspaper in Harrisburg, North Carolina, from May 2006 through 2012. In 2022 and early 2023, she published those newspaper articles in paperback and e-book with the titles *Harrisburg, Did You Know? Cabarrus History, Book 1* and *Harrisburg, Did You Know? Cabarrus History, Book 2*. Those books are available in paperback at Second Look Books in Harrisburg, NC and available in paperback and e-book from Amazon.

Her historical short stories, "Slip Sliding Away" and "Ghost of the Battle of Guilford Courthouse: An American Revolutionary War Ghost Story," were published as standalone books in 2023 and are available in paperback and e-book from Amazon. After that, Janet decided to polish some of the other stories she had written and write some new ones to go along with those two for inclusion in *Traveling Through History: A Collection of Historical Short Stories* in 2025.

Janet's vintage postcard book, *The Blue Ridge Mountains of North Carolina*, was published in 2014 by Arcadia Publishing. It is available in paperback and e-book from Amazon and in paperback from Arcadia Publishing. It is occasionally available at independent bookstores in western North Carolina, or you can request that your favorite bookstore order it for you.

Janet and her sister, Marie Morrison, published a family cookbook in 2023. The title is a play on words that came from a multi-generational tradition in their family. *The Aunts in the Kitchen: Southern Family Recipes* contains recipes from all the aunts in their family. Janet and Marie are now affectionately known as "The Aunts" by their nieces and nephews. It is a moniker they claim with pride. The cookbook includes snippets of information and memories of Janet and Marie's aunts. They were all good cooks! The cookbook is available in paperback at Second Look Books in Harrisburg, NC and from Amazon.

In 1996, Janet and Marie, compiled and published three genealogy books: *Descendants of John & Mary Morrison of Rocky River*; *Descendants of James & Jennet Morrison of Rocky River*; and *Descendants of Robert & Sarah Morrison of Rocky River*. Those hardback books are available through https://www.janetmorrrisonbooks.com.

Janet is writing an historical novel set along the Great Wagon Road in Virginia, North Carolina, and South Carolina in the 1760s. She hopes to write a series of historical novels.

She thanks you for purchasing this collection of short stories and hopes it will bring you hours of enjoyment.

If you are so inclined, she would appreciate your rating or even leaving a short review of this and her other books on Amazon, Goodreads, or other online review venues. Reviews are incredibly valuable to writers, especially when they, like Janet, are trying to establish credibility and name recognition. Thank you for purchasing, reading, reviewing, and telling your friends about this book!

Book descriptions and purchasing information can be found at h ttps://www.janetmorrisonbooks.com. Here is a QR code for your convenience:

Thank you for purchasing *Traveling Through History: A Collection of Historical Short Stories*.